ALL OF US

ALL OF US

A.F. CARTER

HEAD of ZEUS

Originally published in the United States of America in 2020
by The Mysterious Press, an imprint of Grove Atlantic, Inc

First published in the United Kingdom in 2020
by Head of Zeus Ltd
This paperback edition first published in 2021
by Head of Zeus Ltd

9 7 5 3 1 2 4 6 8

A catalogue record for this book is available from
the British Library.

ISBN (PB): 9781838933807
ISBN (E): 9781838933777

Typeset by Divaddict Publishing Solutions Ltd

Printed and bound in Great Britain by
CPI Group (UK) Ltd, Croydon CRO 4YY

FSC www.fsc.org MIX Paper from responsible sources FSC® C020471

Head of Zeus Ltd
5–8 Hardwick Street
London EC1R 4RG

WWW.HEADOFZEUS.COM

ALL OF US

PROLOGUE

When Sergeant Louis Brady pulls up to the intersection of President and Nevins Streets in Brooklyn, he finds three unmarked Ford Escorts, practically his entire squad, haphazardly parked, nose to the curb. Already pissed, he parks his ancient Grand Marquis next to a fire hydrant and gets out. The contrast between the unusually crisp July air and the smoke-saturated interior of the Grand Marquis strikes him immediately, though he's not sure which atmosphere he prefers. He does know that his Vice Unit is out of business in this neighborhood with no arrests to show for the effort. Lieutenant Cathcart will not be happy.

Brady holds up a hand when Patrolman Anthony Ribotta approaches. Brady actively dislikes Ribotta, a Holy Name Society type with a rosary hanging from the rearview mirror of whatever unit he happens to be driving. For cops like Ribotta, a simple prostitution sting can become a crusade to rid the world of impurities. Brady, by contrast, doesn't hate, doesn't even dislike the women and the transvestites he arrests. Take the man's pay, do the man's job, in twenty years comes the magic pension. Brady's entire career is based on this understanding of his role in the war against crime.

Brady waves at the four cops standing by their units. "Tell those bastards to get back to work, Anthony. We can't stay out here all night."

He doesn't wait for a reply but instead approaches the Ford with the woman in the back seat. She's sitting forward on the seat with her knees raised on the seat back in front of her. Her already-short skirt has drifted up, probably when she backed into the car. Now it rides almost at her hips, while her green blouse, sheer to begin with, is unbuttoned far enough to reveal a lacy pink bra that Brady wishes he'd given to his wife last Christmas.

Brady stops a few feet from the car, the sight so wonderfully erotic he wants to prolong it as long as possible. He's assuming the woman is too preoccupied with her situation —she's not handcuffed, but the doors can't be opened or the windows rolled down—to realize she's being watched. But then she turns her head to him, turns it slowly, smiling a sly smile, her green eyes pushing past his baby blues, pushing right down into his brain. Does she find what she's looking for? Brady doesn't know as he watches her turn away, watches her settle onto the seat again, waiting now for whatever comes next.

Brady walks back to where Patrolman Ribotta leans against a streetlight. Ribotta's wearing jeans and a T-shirt with a pocket. He's stuffed a pack of cigarettes into the pocket, a nice touch for an undercover working a sting. Ribotta might be a model for Joe Workingman out for a touch of the strange before heading home to his wife.

"Alright, Anthony, let's hear the story. And keep the bullshit to a minimum."

Ribotta lifts his Yankees cap and runs his hand over his half-inch buzz cut, pushing a little wave of sweat front to back. Then he puts the hat back on and raises his chin, another habit Brady dislikes.

"It's quiet, okay," he begins. "Like so quiet I'm thinkin' the whores know we're out here and they're working some other stroll. But then this woman"—he points to the woman in the back of the car—"she comes walkin' down Nevins Street likes she owns it. Ass and tits, everything moving. I don't know what to think because she doesn't look exactly like a hooker. She's too something I can't put my finger on. But she marches straight up to where I'm standing, no hesitation, Sarge, and propositions me."

"What'd she say?"

"I can't remember exactly. Somethin' about if I have a few hours, I could do her any way I want. Then she said something about eggs."

"Eggs?"

"Yeah, like I could have her sunny-side up or poached or hard-boiled. Whatever I liked."

Brady stares at his subordinate for a moment. Young, tall, good-looking, you dress him up right, he could be working an upscale narcotics sting in a Manhattan bar. "And what'd you do then?"

"My fucking job, Sarge? I asked her how much, but she wasn't hearin' it. Said I was enough reward for a weekday afternoon. I mean, what could I do? She don't take money, she's not a hooker, right? She has to state a price and name an act, this for that. But she wasn't dumb enough to go there."

Here it comes. That's what Brady's thinking. What Patrolman Ribotta should have done is take the lady's phone number and send her on her way. That's exactly what Louis Brady would have done if anything that sweet fell into his lap, which it never has. The woman in the car, though not young, is a real stunner.

"So," Ribotta continues, "I right away figured that something's off here. In the middle of the afternoon you don't proposition a complete stranger on a street known for its hookers unless you got a screw loose somewhere. I mean, she wasn't drunk and didn't look to be stoned, so I just figured she was crazy. And ya know what? I was right. I ran her through NCIC, and she's been locked away twice, once at Creedmoor and once at Brooklyn Psychiatric."

Brady asks two more questions. He wants to settle the facts in his mind. "But she never asked you for money? She never committed a crime?"

"No, Sarge, she's not a hooker. Her name's Carolyn Grand."

Brady spins on his heel. What Ribotta should have done is irrelevant. He, Louis Brady, has become responsible. It's his baby now. He walks back to the Escort, opens the front door, flips the door lock button. Finally, he opens the back door and says, "Why don't you come out of there, Ms. Grand?"

He says it nice, not threatening, because he doesn't want to pack this woman off to the psych unit at Kings County Hospital for three days of observation. Not when the only crime she committed was being stupid enough to proposition Anthony Ribotta.

Carolyn Grand turns her head first. She's smiling, her gaze frank and unafraid, even defiant. Of course, she has to turn her body, tuck in her knees and scoot along the edge of the seat to clear the seat back in front. Which pulls her skirt up even higher. Brady doesn't turn away, but he's not enjoying the show. He's evaluating her readiness to assume responsibility for her own life. Then she does something totally unexpected.

"Please," she says, extending a hand. "Help me out."

Even as he shakes his head no, Brady takes her small hand and gently pulls her to her feet. He's thinking that she's definitely going to try to screw her way out of her predicament, but she freezes instead, her eyes blinking rapidly as her hands flutter over her cheeks and mouth. Then she buttons the front of her blouse and smooths the miniskirt over her thighs, her breathing shallow, her fingers trembling. Finally, her cheeks the red of an overripe tomato, her mouth so tight her lips vanish, she manages to speak a single, barely audible word.

"What?"

Brady shudders. It's like glancing into a mirror only to find someone else glancing back. This mousey woman with the frightened eyes—her neck curled as though she's afraid even to raise her chin, fingers picking at a button on her blouse—this is not the same woman who stared at him from the back seat of the unit, not the woman who slid toward him, her skirt rising to her hips. This is someone else, the transformation rapid enough to leave him with his mouth open.

So, it's no good. No good at all. Brady's first partner, the veteran who broke him in, had made it plain before he put their unit in gear.

"Only one rule, kid, which you should carry with you every day, every minute. Cover your ass. You know why?"

"Why?"

"Because, kid, in the cop world you joined, there's always a foot headed right for it."

Brady recalls the advice even before he asks Carolyn Grand the obvious question. "Why don't you tell me what happened?"

The woman looks down at her feet, hesitating for a moment, but then finds her resolve. "I'm afraid," she tells him, "that I've forgotten."

It's the best she can do, and Brady admires the effort, but it's not enough. He puts her back in the car, then again approaches Ribotta. The woman's nuts, that's for sure, and there's no knowing what she'll do next. Meanwhile, Ribotta ran her name, so there's a record that leads right back to Louis Brady.

"Call in the EMTs, send her to Kings County," he tells Ribotta. "Let the shrinks figure it out."

Brady takes a final look at Carolyn Grand as he heads for his own unit. The look of utter defeat tugs at his heart. He tells himself that if he's wrong, if she's not crazy, she'll only spend a day or two at Kings County. No big deal, right? But some tours of duty, as Brady learned many years before, are worse than others. Some tours are worse than others and some tours are fucking impossible.

CHAPTER ONE
VICTORIA

I take a second to adjust my game face—I should say we, because there are others watching—before I open the door and step into Dr. Halberstam's office. It's four days since we were discharged from a locked psych ward at Kings County Hospital and our appearance is a condition of our discharge. Do it or else.

I find our therapist standing behind his desk, his expression as composed as my own. He says, "Good morning, Ms. Grand, please have a seat."

I accept the chair he offers, though I would have preferred another. The back of this chair is tilted. I can't sit up straight unless I perch on the edge. Nor can I walk out of his office, which I and my sisters and my brother would most like to do. I'm stuck here, forced into a posture, if not seductive, at least vulnerable. For the present, Dr. Laurence Halberstam owns us. I know it, and he knows it.

I watch him sit behind his desk, his chair back far more upright than mine. I watch him shuffle through the case file on his desk, our case file: thick, substantial, the history of our lives as told by the many therapists and psychologists and psychiatrists who've dissected us over the past twenty years.

"Well, Ms. Grand—"

I stop him with a small shake of my head. "There's no Ms. Grand, Doctor, and there hasn't been for many years. There's only us." I can afford to be open here because I'm not telling him anything he doesn't already know. "I want to be frank," I claim, "right from the beginning."

His expression doesn't change, but I didn't expect it to. Our therapist is in his midforties, with a slender body and a full head of neatly parted hair that I suspect to be his pride and joy. Every hair is in place, every strand uniformly black. There's not a hint of gray, or even a thinning on top when he bends forward to study his notes, taking his time about it. He wears a gray suit over a starched blue shirt and a muted red tie. The tie's Windsor knot forms a perfect triangle beneath his chin, but the tie itself is slightly askew, an imperfection that somehow pleases me.

Without changing expression, he lifts his head and looks at me, a technique we've encountered several times in the past. Still, I have to concede Halberstam's mastery of the silent stare. His blue eyes are piercing, even behind the glasses. Finally, he says, "Can I assume that I'm talking to Victoria?"

Presenting an acceptable public face is my job, my function. I represent the family, the four girls and one boy who share this body. In that capacity, I'm required to project, first and foremost, that our situation is under control. Which it's not, of course, which it's never been, as my siblings are quick to remind me when I'm too full of myself. Still, I'm wearing my demure best, a full, brown skirt that falls to within two inches of my knees, a white blouse with a scalloped collar and a tan sweater. My shoulder-length hair has been swept back to cover my ears. Except for a light coating of dark red lipstick, I'm not wearing makeup.

"And where are the others," Halberstam asks, his tone studiously neutral. "Right this minute?"

"Some watching, some wherever."

"That's interesting. Who would you say is watching? And why?"

As I compose myself, I glance around Halberstam's office. We've passed time in many psych offices, enough to know they fall into three general patterns. The warm and cozy, the ultrahip, the cool, calm, and collected. Halberstam's office fits the latter category. Beige wallpaper, a lacquered desk that reflects my shins, hints of mauve in the chairs, porcelain and pottery in lit niches. LED lights frame the outer edges of the ceiling, while a desk lamp with an amber shade provides the only real color in the room.

The décor advertises Halberstam's approach. He will be neither friend nor foe. He will play the part of the objective observer, his goal to help us help ourselves. Sadly, we've generally done better with the homey types, the huggers.

"Martha, of course, and Tina. They're watching."

"And the others? Where are they?"

I shrug. "Wherever."

He's not having it, and he gets right to the point. We don't exist and never will. "Where do you go, Victoria, when you're not in control and not watching?"

"Well, that's the question, isn't it? And I apologize for not having an answer, except to say we don't relate well to clock time. It seems to me that I exist at every moment, but I know that can't be strictly accurate."

"And why is that?"

"Because there are periods of time I can't account for, long periods of time. But, then again, where does your anger go, Doctor, when you're not angry? Your laughter, your hunger, your thirst?"

I watch his eyes narrow. My feeble challenge has annoyed him and he'll try to put me in my place. To prove the point, he asks a question I think he was saving for later on.

"Describe the incident that brought you here. Or better yet, perhaps you can summon the identity who precipitated your encounter with the police."

"That would be Eleni. She's not around, and I have no way to reach her. As for summoning?" I pause long enough to smile. In the movies, split personality types call their various identities into consciousness at will. If only that were true, our lives would be a lot easier. "The truth, Doctor, is that we have no central identity to do the summoning. If Eleni were observing, there's a chance she would appear spontaneously. But she's in hiding, in disgrace, hopefully repenting for the monumental screwup that put us in this position."

"That's fine, Victoria. Just tell me what you know. Eleni and I will meet later on."

Do I detect the beginnings of a leer? Because we could live with the sexual interest, a natural consequence of a childhood passed in bondage to a sexual sadist who liked to entertain his friends. Eleni, especially, would be eager to accept the challenge, assuming there's a deal in the offing.

"All right, I'll describe the events as best I can. Eleni? Well, she has a theory. Bodies have needs. There are the obvious, of course, to eat, drink, breathe, and sleep. But there are others as well, including sex. Eleni has decided—"

"On her own? Against your will?"

"Very much against my will."

Suddenly, Eleni's mocking laughter—maybe she's been listening all along—rolls through my brain. I'm a virgin, by inclination and necessity, and Eleni never loses an opportunity to remind me.

"Go on, please."

"Eleni has chosen to provide for this need."

"Does she have a lover?"

Should I tell him the truth? Do I have a choice? Halberstam's surely read the police report. Like any good lawyer, he knew the answer to his question before he posed it. For all Eleni's pretense, she's a reckless fool who's never met a risk she didn't want to take. Her preference, over the last few years, has been for drug-fueled hookups, often with multiple partners. More than once I've reclaimed our body only to find it bruised and battered.

"Eleni is promiscuous, Doctor. Six days ago, she traveled from our Brooklyn apartment to an area on the waterfront notorious for street prostitution." I take a breath, utterly humiliated. Just words, I tell myself, just words.

"Go on."

"Well, she propositioned a man standing outside a bodega who turned out to be an undercover cop working a prostitution sting. I don't know what she said, but as she never asked for money, she couldn't be charged with a crime. Still, something in her manner, in her words, in her dress activated the cop's radar, and he decided that he was dealing with an EDP."

"An emotionally disturbed person?"

"Exactly."

A red light flashes on the intercom to the left of Halberstam's notes. He glances at it for a moment, then turns back to me. "I'm afraid our time is almost up, but please describe what came next."

"We were taken to Kings County Hospital for observation." By then, Eleni had fled the scene, leaving me to handle the inconvenience. Wearing, of course, the slutty outfit she'd chosen for her excursion. "Prior to our mandatory hearing three days later, we were poked and prodded by psychiatrists and psychologists in one-on-one and group sessions. We were tested as well, with objective tests, projective tests, attitude tests. We even took what the examiner called an EPES test, an Erotic Preferences Examination Scheme."

I don't have to state the purpose of all this testing because the issue was and remains simple. Are we fit to live independently? Or does the danger we present to ourselves or to the public justify indefinite confinement—accompanied by a regimen of psychoactive drugs, many of which have a sedating effect that leaves our body's multiple personalities with no personality at all.

Psychiatric hospitals are not prisons. So it's said, especially by the politicians and medical personnel who run them. They just look and function like prisons. The doors are locked, and you exercise, sleep, and eat on a schedule you play no part in creating. True, the women on your ward usually aren't criminals. Instead, three-quarters are either schizophrenic or bipolar. Despite the sedating medications, they howl, scream, bawl, and beg at every hour of the day and night. Patient-on-patient attacks are commonplace.

When I finally walked our body out of the psych ward at Kings County Hospital four days ago, I felt like I'd escaped death itself.

If so, that escape was tenuous. Our court-appointed attorney, Mark Vernon, had pulled no punches when he spelled it out only a few days before: "This is not a trial, Ms. Grand. It's a medical hearing and many of the protections afforded defendants at trial are unavailable. Do you need to be protected from yourself? Doctors will examine you and doctors will ultimately decide. It's a rare judge who'll override a recommendation from the medical community."

"May I sum up?" Halberstam asks, yanking me away from my thoughts.

"Certainly."

"You've been granted a conditional release dependent on your entering into therapy. I've been assigned the task of conducting that therapy. You know this, right?"

"Yes, I do."

I watch his eyes narrow slightly, a shift mirrored by his small, thin mouth. He's about to assert his rightful authority as he leans forward to place his palms on his desk, as he tucks in his chin, as he peers over his glasses.

"I know your therapy has been forced on you. I know that you're probably resentful and not without reason. But while I'm not a fan of coercive therapy, we are stuck with each other, which means in essence that only a short time from now I will be required to submit a recommendation to the court. I must choose, at that point, between three possibilities: return you to your ordinary life, continue your therapy, or recommend that you be confined. I'm hoping to make an informed choice and not an educated guess, which I cannot do unless I become acquainted with each of your identities."

There's nothing to be said here except: "I understand."

"That's good, Victoria." He rises, our session now complete. "I'll expect you tomorrow at ten a.m. and every weekday thereafter. We've a lot to go through before I make my recommendation."

I can hear Martha's voice offering advice, as usual. "Keep your mouth shut," she tells me. "And get the hell out of there. Begging will do you no good."

But I can't stop myself. "I know it looks bad, Doctor. I mean Eleni and what she did. But we've been reintegrating for years. Jackson, Logan, Riley, Aria, and Chloe? They're gone, Doctor, banished. Others are on their way out. It's a hard path we're on, but we're moving. If you can help us, all the better. We want to unify."

"Each of you? Every one?"

A gotcha question, but I'm ready this time. "Those who don't will be eliminated. They'll be the first to go."

CHAPTER TWO
MARTHA

As I come out of the shower, I stop before a full-length mirror to examine our thirty-seven-year-old body. It's an attractive body we share. Sexy enough for Eleni's purposes anyway. But arousal's not on my schedule. No, I'm fascinated by the scars—our legacy—the perfectly round cigarette burns on our abdomen. A spider's web of thin white lines that could only have been made by a razor-sharp blade. There are other scars, too, but they only show up on X-rays.

I have no memory of my father, now in prison, or of his sadistic friends. Nor do I remember Benny Aceveda and his wife, the foster parents who rented us out by the hour. I can't picture these assholes. I wouldn't recognize them if they walked into the room and farted. That's not my job. That task belongs to our rememberer-in-chief, Tina. It's not fair to put this on a girl who will remain nine years old forever. But we're not some academic paper on functional psychology. We're not some bullshit theory. We're real and the proof is Tina, herself. That she exists. That she suffers. That despite everything, she hopes to survive.

Our past is imprinted somewhere inside the brain we share, but Tina alone has access. If that saves the rest of us a lot of pain, the arrangement has a serious downside. Tina's attempted to kill herself twice. The last time, only six months ago, she came very close to solving our problems once and for all. Fortunately, we woke up in our own bed. No cops, no hospital, no doctor. All in the family.

I'm not much interested in our past this morning and my inspection of our body is cursory. I'm Martha, family functioner. Without me, the rest of the assholes wouldn't have food on the table, clothes on their backs, a roof over their heads. They wouldn't have electricity or a telephone or toilet paper.

Victoria, if you talk to her, will claim that she's the one who got us on disability, food stamps, Medicaid, and a Section 8 rent subsidy. The four engines of our economic survival. The only problem is that she's full of shit. Yeah, she went to the interviews (and did a good job), but I filled out every form and there were hundreds. I also made the necessary calls when things went wrong, as they usually did. And I kept track of the bureaucrats, their names, their phone numbers. And I wrote the goddamned appeals and deposited the checks and created our tight, tight budget. And I'm still the one who pushes a shopping cart over to the food bank when no amount of budgeting can turn our monthly fifteen hundred dollars into a living income.

What I am, when I think about it, is a nasty old lady trapped in a young woman's body. (Not the worst, really. My brother,

Kirk, is a heterosexual male trapped in a woman's body. His few friends think he's a dyke.) Still, bottom line, joy is not part of my game plan. I'm a drudge, by necessity and inclination. This is my value, toilet paper on the roll in the bathroom, a clean towel hanging on the rack, a shiny white sink. I know it—we all know it—but at least I'm not a pompous asshole. Like Victoria.

Today is laundry day at the Grand residence, a tiny apartment in a crumbling Fort Greene tenement. I grab the laundry basket, empty the hamper, change the sheets in the bedroom. The same routine tasks that none of the others will do. Instead, they toss their clothes on the floor and leave dishes in every room. If I didn't clean up and go heavy on the Combat, it'd be cockroach heaven up here. As it is, I trap a mouse in the apartment at least once a week.

Changing the sheets on our bed isn't as simple as it seems because the room is barely wide enough for the bed frame. There's not even space for a night table and I have to wiggle my way down to the head of the bed, my ass jammed against the wall. I'm about halfway down when someone knocks on the door in the other room.

I think I know who it is. Our deal with Section 8 requires us to pay $200 a month toward the rent, our $1,500 income ($1,400 from disability and $100 in food stamps) too grand for a total subsidy. In New York City, housing crisis capital of the goddamned world.

Our check from disability is direct deposited into our checking account on the first Wednesday of each month. That can be as late as the sixth when the rent's due on the first. My landlord is aware of this, but he always sends Doyle, his scumbag super, to break balls. Doyle instinctively realizes there's something wrong with us. He's been at the door too many times, met too many of us. That includes Eleni, who blew him off for the pitiful jerk he is.

I open the door, but it's not Doyle. It's a black woman about my age extending an ID from the Human Resources Administration.

"Ms. Portman," she announces. "From Adult Protective Services."

My hand, the one on the door, twitches. That's how much I want to slam the door in her face. I pretty much dislike everyone—Victoria insists that I'm not fit for human company—but I actually hate bureaucrats. We come to them as beggars and they never let us forget it. Or lose an opportunity to display their power over us.

I make it as simple as possible: "What do you want?"

"To inspect your apartment."

"Just like that?"

Portman shakes her head. She's tall and thin, wearing a midnight-blue pants suit over a lavender blouse. An expensive leather briefcase hangs from a shoulder strap. When she speaks, her tone is sympathetic yet firm. So sorry, but step aside.

"The inspection is court mandated," she tells me.

"And that gives you the right to come here without calling ahead?"

Her lips move, but she doesn't speak for a moment. I know she's choosing her words, but, again, her tone is not unkind.

"I'm not your enemy," she claims. "Our mission at Protective Services is to protect. That means evaluating your everyday living conditions, which doesn't work if I call you in advance."

"What if there was no one ho—" I have to close my eyes for a moment as Doyle appears at the head of the stairs. The moron's wearing his customary T-shirt and a pair of faded jeans belted across fifty pounds of quivering blubber. He's flashing his customary smirk, too. Displaying a row of large, nicotine-yellow teeth behind a pair of wet lips.

"What the hell is that?" Portman asks.

I glance at her, noting the faint smile on her face. "That's Doyle, the super. He's after the rent."

"You've fallen behind?"

"Yeah, four days."

The farce intensifies when the door across the hall opens to reveal Marshal, my neighbor. He steps into the hallway, closely followed by a cloud of marijuana smoke. Marshal's apartment is usually Kirk's first stop when he's in control of our body. Nevertheless, Marshal is hard not to like. He's a dedicated slacker who supports himself by selling small amounts of weed, a thirty-year-old boy obsessed with the electronic music he creates in his bedroom.

"Hey, what's happening," he mutters as he heads for the staircase. Doyle, an aspiring slacker himself, turns and follows.

"Yo, Marshal, got a minute."

* * *

"Another morning at Chez Nazari," I explain. Our building, our home, was named Chez Nazari by a defunct identity. Muhammad Nazari is our bastard of a landlord. He's adopted a simple business model. Provide only the most basic services (every ten days or so, his tenants go without hot water) and evict tenants whenever possible. Our building is rent stabilized, so the rents go up slowly, if at all. On the other hand, the law authorizes a 20 percent jump whenever an apartment becomes vacant. Throw in a few bullshit improvements and you can easily get to 30 percent. Turnover is the name of the game.

The disgusted expression on Portman's round face as she surveys the corridor's peeling walls tells me all I need to know. I gesture for her to enter and she saunters through the doorway. We catch a lucky break here. I've been piloting our body since early last night and the apartment's in good order, which is not always the case.

Portman's taller than me by a good three inches. I follow in her wake as she conducts her inspection. Feeling the way I feel when I watch our body perform and I'm not in charge.

"These are lovely," she says, indicating a half dozen flower arrangements. The flowers are artificial, the arrangements courtesy of Serena, our resident artiste. They're quite restrained, single blossoms mostly, surrounded by narrow leaves and a sprig of berries or a trailing vine. From somewhere deep inside, I hear Serena stir. She'll want to know why I didn't mention her name.

Portman's thorough. Not content with a clean living room and kitchen, she examines the refrigerator, the kitchen cabinets and the oven before checking under the sink. I can almost hear her mind working: *Bleach, check; laundry detergent, check; floor cleaner, check.*

Meticulous or not, Portman's done inside of ten minutes. We've basically got a two-room apartment with a turnaround kitchen and a bathroom so small the toilet touches the side of the tub. Our sparse furnishings and most of the prints on the walls were rescued from the trash on garbage pickup day.

It goes without saying that nothing in our apartment matches anything else. The four wooden chairs around the dining table, for just one example, are not only different shapes but also different colors. Still, I know Portman's not fazed by our poverty. Impoverished households are as familiar to her as waking up in the morning. She's a poverty connoisseur.

"Looks good," she announces. "So, I guess that's it. I don't see anything that merits our attention."

I should leave it there, but I can't. "Excuse me, but I'm trying to understand what exactly we did to warrant all this attention."

"I've been wondering myself. The court ordered Protective Services to make this inspection and file a report. We weren't provided with a reason and have no choice except to comply. That said, if the rest of the inquiry goes as well as this inspection, our report will be positive."

"The rest of the inquiry?"

"Well, we still have to talk to your neighbors."

CHAPTER THREE
SERENA

So stunning, to be alive, to be outdoors, a simple pedestrian, no more and no less than any pedestrian on any street in New York, an absolute equal marching down a city street on a spring day with a warm southerly breeze carrying the primitive scent of the harbor. No trees here, no flowers or green, surging grass, no bunny rabbits, frolicking fawns, instead practical, always-in-a-hurry city folk, instead old men and women inching their way along, instead destitute and desperate panhandlers talking to themselves, eyes locked into their own madness. Four adolescent boys evaluate my sexual potential, their energy washing over my body, adding to the scream of an advancing ambulance. Eyes down, skirt falling to her ankles, a woman in a black hijab pushes a crying child in a stroller. A small, white dog squats at the curb, owner hovering above, poop bag at the ready.

The universe flows down Fulton Street, everything connected, every tendril in place, until there are no pieces, only one chord, each note sung, even the trash in the street, the buzzing sign above the entrance to Crunch gym, the hiss of released air as a bus pulls away from the curb, a true plainsong, proof everlasting of our creators at play. I take joy in the knowledge, the certainty, the evidence as plainly displayed as the exhibits at a murder trial: rope, restraints, knife, handsaw, the collective gaze of shaken jurors as they dutifully examine photos taken after the body was finally discovered.

Fulton Street evolves as I head south, penetrating the gentrified neighborhoods closer to Brooklyn Heights and the bridge. Faces and bodies flow effortlessly past, words bounce against my ears: Arabic, Spanish, Russian. A Hasidic couple passes, arguing in Yiddish, the words tangle with Martha's entreaties, her pragmatism another note, only adding to the perpetual harmony.

"Halberstam, Halberstam, Halberstam, appointment, appointment, appointment . . ."

A cold, wet mop, never knowing even the ecstasy of Eleni, the physical release, the surrender to whatever consciousness-altering substance happens to be available and to the ultimate threat arising from casual sex with strangers. I pause to inspect a fruit vendor's long table, the yellows and greens and oranges, a soft, soft peach, fuzz bristling, all caught in the revealing light of a perfect sun, a pure gold disc in a pure blue sky.

I buy an apple from a turbaned vendor with a triangular black beard and eat it as I turn on to Boerum Place, now called Brooklyn Bridge Boulevard, the street renamed for tourists who add their own essentials to the collective scent. I feel them around me, that we share a common goal, the still-shielded bridge rising just beyond a long curve, a yearning for the heights. Victoria and Martha want to eat me, me and Eleni, to swallow us down, to digest us, to empty us from their bowels, to flush us away. That in so doing they abandon their futures, consigning themselves to an empty survival, no joy, no love, no ecstasy, troubles them not at all. I hurry along, moving with a river of humans, the bridge a vacuum drawing us into its center, the force irresistible, up the promenade, between a spider's web of intersecting cables, to the great arches where I press my hands against a massive block of rough-hewn stone. Two bridges cross the East River to the north, ahead the great towers present a solid front to would-be invaders, Lady Liberty stands, a solitary figure on a lonely pedestal in the harbor to the south, resolute.

CHAPTER FOUR
MARTHA

I'm running like a fool. Like the pitiful mental case we are. Tourists stare at me and speeding cyclists pass close enough to brush my arm. I pay no attention, there being only room in my brain for two thoughts. First, I'm going to be late for the fourth appointment with our shithead of a therapist. Victoria kept the first three, hoping the good doctor would let us off the hook with a cursory inspection. Not happening. He expects to meet all of us at some point. Especially Eleni, our main offender.

So, there's that bullshit to handle. But there's also a burning rage because my free-spirit sister has done it again. In the past, Serena regularly hijacked our body as we headed off to work. She liked to take us on spiritual journeys certain to get us fired. The girl believes herself to be an artist and a poet and a pilgrim. In fact, she's a fucking moron.

I dodge pedestrians all the way to the foot of the bridge, then run alongside city hall to the Brooklyn Bridge subway station. I get lucky for once and a 6 Train pulls into the station as I pass through the turnstile. There are no seats, but I don't care. I stand in the center of the car, one hand clutching a pole that runs floor to ceiling. I'm wearing a white peasant blouse and a brown, wraparound skirt speckled with gold rabbits. This is Serena's favorite summertime outfit, but it doesn't work for a self-proclaimed drudge. Nor does the loosened hair that cascades to my shoulders, or the almost-black lipstick, or the peacock-blue eye shadow.

In fact, I look like an idiot, a complete asshole, a total phony. Like Serena with her beads and her artificial flowers pretending she's an artist. If we're ever to have control of our lives, Victoria and I, we need to kick Serena to the curb. Eleni, too. We need to dump the both of them.

But that's not going to happen anytime soon. And it won't happen fast, either. The others went only after a long crusade. We froze them out, abandoned them, the parting not without pain, yet ultimately satisfying. Like pulling an infected tooth.

We'd been taking us for granted before unity was even a goal. Then we met Dr. Charlotte Harmon, the first therapist to fully understand our dilemma. We'd created us out of necessity she insisted. Which was fine. Carolyn had to escape and creating identities with no memory of the nightmare she'd endured was a brilliant solution. Her response was that of a sane child dealing with an insane environment. But circumstances change over time and us was not a strategy suitable to our present or future, no matter how well adapted it might have been to our past. We needed a plan B.

Dr. Harmon reached us (most of us, anyway) precisely because she didn't think we were crazy.

* * *

I stand in the corridor outside Halberstam's office for several minutes before I turn the knob. I need to ease off the gas and I tell myself that we've been here. I mean subject to a man with power. Be mostly honest. Don't lose your temper.

Victoria's with me this morning as I turn the doorknob and I sense an almost-hidden presence behind her. Kirk, our little boy-girl. Like Eleni, like Serena, Kirk's a must-go.

Halberstam's waiting room is as drab as Victoria's description of his inner office, more beige on beige. That includes a middle-aged receptionist named Tanya who wears a beige jacket over a beige skirt. I take a seat and glance at a magazine, *People*, but don't pick it up. I'm not expecting a long delay, being as I'm fifteen minutes late.

Tanya presses a button on the intercom, then leans forward and whispers something into the machine. Finally, she turns to me, her expression grave. "You may go in now," she intones.

Victoria described Halberstam's gaze as intense, but I find it evaluating. The kind of look a cheetah might bestow on a herd of gazelles before choosing a victim. But he's not looking at me when I enter the room. He's turned to one side, offering his angular profile while he scans a document.

I take a seat in the chair assigned to us and lean back, the sensation as unpleasant as it is submissive. Halberstam appears not to notice, but his disinterest seems to me theatrical. I don't react because we're accustomed to the scrutiny of therapists and know their techniques must be endured.

The only therapists who've done us any good have been female. Take it to the bank. And while I have no sex life of my own, I know that if I ever go down that road, it will be with a woman.

Halberstam finally straightens in his very upright chair. "You're late," he says.

There's nothing to be gained by lying and I don't try. "The body," I explain, "was hijacked as I began to dress for the appointment. By the time I regained control . . ." I shrug, the message plain enough.

"And who did the hijacking?"

"Serena, our free spirit."

"And when this hijacking occurred, you were helpless to prevent it? You couldn't refuse?"

Halberstam's just verbalized the essence of our problem. Which the jerk surely knew before he posed the question. I supply him with an answer prepared in advance. Tit for tat.

"If Carolyn Grand had a central authority who could order her identities, you would never have known she existed. That's because she'd be sane." I pause for a moment, then jump through the required hoop. "We've never done the choosing, Doctor, not from the day we were born."

"Fine, in fact undeniable." Halberstam leans back and crosses his legs. "Tell me. How do you know that Serena hijacked the body? Why not Victoria?"

I hate the role I'm in, unavoidable or not. I don't see why I should have to explain anything to this moron. I don't see why I should have to endure the semi-sneer that passes for a smile. Submission has never been my strong point.

Something inside me, perhaps one of the others, demands that I lie. Tell him you know it was Serena because the clothes you're wearing could only belong to her. The truth will not set you free.

I ignore the advice. "I know, Doctor, because I was there. Along for the ride."

"Just the two of you?"

"This time."

"And other times?"

"Any number, any combination. It's always been that way." I reflect for just a second. Then I repeat myself. "Always."

"So, you've never questioned this arrangement?"

I take a second to adjust my thoughts, then say, "Look, Doctor. Early on I questioned every arrangement. Especially the most basic, who and what I am. But what's the point? I can't will myself into or out of existence, so I take what I can get. Like the rest of us."

Halberstam replies a bit too fast. "Well said. Lack of control is the essence of your problem, a point also made by Victoria." He folds his hands and lays them on the desk as he fixes me with one of those penetrating stares. "May I ask who I'm speaking to?"

"You're speaking to Martha."

"And how would you describe your . . . your role, Martha?"

"Old-fashioned housewife. I cook, clean, shop, pay the bills. I keep our little household up and running."

"Victoria plays no part?"

"She does face-to-face. When we have to be seen." Like my sister, I have no problem switching from "we" to "I" and back again. "Apart from taking out the garbage and collecting the mail, I try to keep my head down."

"Can you tell me why?"

"I have a short fuse. I don't really like people."

"Would you call yourself a misanthrope?"

"I might if I knew what it meant." My tone is sharp enough to be confused with sarcasm, one of those errors I vowed not to make. I watch Halberstam nod. I'm about to be punished.

"Do you remember what happened to you when you were a child?"

"No, I have no direct memory of my childhood. Carolyn Grand was twenty-five when I first became aware."

"But you do know what happened, even if you can't remember?"

"Yes, Doctor, I do know. And I'm reminded every time I step out of the shower and count the scars on my body."

"The physical abuse." His tone is eager and he's leaning forward. "Victoria was very forthcoming about the physical abuse, but the other part, the sexual abuse . . . like you, she claimed to be totally unfamiliar with that phase of Carolyn Grand's life."

"Like I already said, Victoria and I were born on the same day, a week after Carolyn's twenty-fifth birthday."

Halberstam waves me off. His features are relaxed now, relaxed and confident. "Your father made movies, Martha, made them and sold them, movies that still circulate among pedophiles. You've seen these movies, so your childhood cannot be as remote as you make it out to be."

Fifteen years ago, one of our therapists, Dequan Cho, decided that it was time that we confronted our past. We'd been running away for years, he explained, and look where we ended up. Our desperate attempt to escape a past that couldn't be escaped had left us at the mercy of psychological forces we'd never vanquish. Not unless we confronted that past, unless we acknowledged the damage done to us. How? By reviewing some of the movies made by our father.

Cho had a combative personality. Fight, fight, fight. He'd grown up a privileged child in Riverdale and didn't have a clue about the effect of that footage on poor Tina. Tina had been the star of those movies. Coerced into them by her father, Hank Grand, a malignant narcissist who loved to hurt the people closest to him. And nobody was closer than his daughter.

Unfortunately, Cho's suggestion wasn't a suggestion. We were guests of the state, restricted to a locked ward at Creedmoor Psychiatric Center after a now-banished identity took a nap on the Long Island Expressway. Life was crazy then. Identities came and went so fast it was like flipping through a deck of cards. Victoria and I weren't around at that time, only Kirk, the oldest of us. He wanted out of Creedmoor—desperately, desperately, desperately, as Serena would say—and so he and the others agreed to watch.

Cho played the movies, maybe a dozen in all, for many hours over the next ten days. And I have to suppose our cooperation made a difference because Cho released us a few months later. Kirk and the rest were euphoric—free at last—and they might have remained euphoric if Tina hadn't made her first attempt at suicide a week later. It took a day and a half to clean up the blood.

"The movies were unbearable, Doctor. But that's only what was told to me by Kirk. The rest of us, except for Tina, had yet to be born."

Halberstam spun a pen on his desk for a moment, the flick of his fingers so precise the pen described a perfect circle. I watched his tongue swish over his lips, but when he looked at me again, I saw only indifference in his gaze.

"Let's talk for a moment about the incident that preceded your confinement at Kings County Hospital. One of your identities, I believe her name is Eleni, made an obscene proposal to a stranger. Do you think she meant to follow through? If the man agreed?"

Victoria's as outraged as I am. I know Eleni considers me a prude, but that's not remotely true. If she'd only be discreet. If she'd stop coming home with STDs, stop using whatever drug her partners chose to share, she could indulge her perverted desires from night until morning. There's no moral issue here, not as far as I'm concerned.

I have a response to Halberstam's question prepared, just not the one Victoria and I agreed on. "You have a computer on your desk, Doctor. Do a Google search for 'swinger clubs in NYC.' You'll find page after page, club after club, many open to couples only. And if you search a little more, you'll find agencies dedicated to making your deviant sexual fantasies come true. Just tell 'em what you want and they'll arrange it. Craigslist, as well. Anything you want. Now, tell me, how many of the men and women who took advantage of the ads were threatened with involuntary commitment as a result?"

Halberstam only smiles. "The incident that brought Eleni to the attention of the police didn't take place inside a club and it wasn't arranged by an agency. It happened on a public street, stranger to stranger. The inherent risk is obvious."

"Really?" I'm going too fast now, but I can't stop thinking about all those construction workers who make sucking noises when an attractive woman passes by. "How many young men and women do you think visited the bars and clubs in Manhattan last Saturday? How many sought casual sex? How many went home with a stranger? They call them hookups, Doctor, and they happen thousands of times every weekend. But nobody goes to jail because they want to get laid. Except us."

"Kings County Hospital is not a jail. It's an ordinary hospital with a short-term psychiatric facility. In addition, you haven't been charged with a crime and you won't be. In fact, I'll probably recommend that your therapy continue long enough for me to fully understand your situation and formulate a course of treatment. I hope things go well, of course."

Halberstam smiles at that moment, perhaps expecting me to express my eternal gratitude despite the implied threat. That won't happen because life under Halberstam's thumb will include the fear, more or less constant, that we can still be committed. That it's up to him.

"That works for us," I say.

"Excellent. Now, you were late today, and I understand why. But I can't have you perpetually late or skipping sessions altogether. And I must become acquainted with each of your identities, including Eleni and"—he glances at his notes—"and Tina, the young one. You've said that individual identities can't be ordered to appear and I believe you. But I'm hoping you can work on it."

"We'll do what we can, Victoria and I."

"Excellent." Halberstam looks down at his watch. "Well, we got a late start and our session is at an end. But there is one other thing and I'm going to put the matter bluntly. I only found out this morning, but your father will be paroled in less than a week."

I can't process the information at first, and I stammer, "What, what, what?"

"You were ten years old when Henry Grand was sentenced to thirty years in prison for what he did to you and many others. He's now served twenty-seven. I don't have any details, not yet, but he obviously convinced a parole board that he no longer poses a significant threat to the community. In any event, there's nothing you or I can do except deal with it in the course of your therapy." He gestures at the door. "I'll reach out to the parole board for more details tomorrow morning. More than likely, some kind of restraining order will be issued. Now, if you'll be so kind."

As the door closes behind me, I hear Eleni's voice in my ear. "Thanks," she says, "for standin' up for me."

CHAPTER FIVE
KIRK

I roll out of bed at three o'clock, in sole possession of the body, everyone else asleep. Yea, team. I yank on my usual costume, gray sweats, top and bottom, and a navy watch cap to cover my too-long hair. Then I'm out the door.

I don't get much time with the body and tonight I need to make the most of it. That's because I'm convinced that Halberstam is more than an asshole therapist. The scumbag's running a game and I can't see us sitting on our collective butts until we know what it is. That sick-ass look in his eye when he told Martha about our father's parole? Behind the glasses, underneath the gleam, I saw a little boy, a happy, happy little boy.

A long-term psychiatric hospital is little more than a prison. The biggest difference? There's no definite sentence, no time to be served after which you must be released. You can be held for a month or for the rest of your miserable, shitty life. Any stumble is your own fault because you are, by definition, your own worst enemy. Else why the fuck would you be here?

Bottom line, you're doin' it to yourself and you need to stop. Or maybe submit to a twice-daily dose of Clozapine and spend the hours with drool runnin' down your chin, your heart rate so fast you think your chest's about to explode.

Eleni's on my side, Serena, too. But not the prunes, Victoria and Martha. If they knew what I was doing, they'd try to stop me. Just like they're doin' everything they can to get rid of me. Maybe they're afraid I'll grow a cock and leave them, for a change, the odd girls out. Just like I've been the odd boy out for years and years and years. My rare lovers confined to lesbians who think I'm a woman.

I leave the apartment, cross the hallway and knock on Marshal's door. It takes a few minutes but he finally answers, bleary eyed. He's wearing royal-blue boxers and a Sex Pistols T-shirt with GOD SAVE THE QUEEN written across Queen Elizabeth's face. No socks, no shoes.

"Hey, Kirk, wha'sup?"

"Need a few minutes, man."

"Cool." He steps back to let me pass, then follows me inside. Marshal knows all about us, from me and from Eleni, who's hauled his ashes a few times. He doesn't care. Simple as that. Marshal may be a loser, but he's also the most accepting human being on the planet.

"Sorry to get in your business this late," I tell him as I find a seat between the lumps on his couch. "But I don't get around much anymore."

"Yeah, Duke Ellington."

"Huh."

"'Don't Get Around Much Anymore.' Duke Ellington wrote the tune. Back in the day."

I'm supposed to recognize Duke Ellington's name. Marshal's tone makes that much clear. Everyone's supposed to recognize Duke Ellington's name. But I don't.

"You want a beer? You wanna hit the bong?" Marshal asks. "Both maybe?"

Actually, what I really want to do is run over to a club I know on West Twenty-Eighth Street, a lezzie hangout where I pass for a dyke.

"Let's have a hit on the bong."

"A hit or ten." Marshal's thirty years old, still young, but his scraggly beard is already turning gray. "Why limit your future before it happens?"

I lean back in the couch as Marshal prepares the bong. I don't have to guess about the quality of his weed because it's always the same, good but not great. Marshal's been selling ganja for more than a decade and he's got enough loyal customers to keep a roof over his head, food in the refrigerator, clothes on his back. So what if there's nothing left at the end of the month? Marshal once told me that he doesn't let himself want anything he doesn't already have.

Marshal loads the bong and passes it to me, along with a little torch. Five minutes later, I'm blissed out.

"Hey, Marshal, you once told me about your business." I gesture to the bong. "Where you buy, remember? Somethin' about the dark web?"

"Yeah, so what—"

"Well, I'm not prying, bro. I got a reason for asking, so if you'd refresh my memory . . ."

Marshal pauses long enough to hit the bong. He holds the smoke in his lungs for a minute, then blows it toward the ceiling.

"Hey, man, this bit about the dark web, which is actually the deep web? That shit is way over the top. Like, it's just a lot of websites that haven't been indexed, so they can't be found by a search engine. Mostly, the sites belong to private clubs or managers in a large company. Just for example, VPs at Exxon don't use the public website, the one you can find with a Google search, to communicate. They have a web address that's not indexed. So, what I'm saying is that most of the deep web is legit. Only a small percentage of sites operate illegally."

I smile. "And that's where you come in?"

"What could I say, Kirk? I send an email that can't be traced back to me because it's encrypted at least three times by a virtual private network. I send it to a computer that might be anywhere on the planet and two days later I get a delivery, usually from a man or woman I've never seen before. No guns, no threats, no fucking paranoia. It's the new way."

Marshal's nodding happily because he's found the sweet spot. If his suppliers get busted and turn snitch, they have to rat up the ladder, not down to him. As for his own customers, he sells them half ounces in a city where a half ounce isn't even a misdemeanor. No, the only thing Marshal really fears is legalization. Which is on the way.

"So, Kirk, what's up? I know you're here for somethin' specific, so spit it out. If I can help . . ."

I describe what I need as best I can. On my own, when it comes to computers, I can barely get online. Victoria's pretty good, but my siblings and I don't necessarily share memories. For example, Martha is a great cook, but Eleni has trouble boiling water. We don't know why this is true, but there it is, another stacked card in a stacked deck.

"Acquirin' what you want, my man, is not gonna be your biggest problem," Marshal finally says. "The problem's gonna be installing the malware into another computer."

"I'll worry about that later. You say you can get me what I want?"

"Yeah, definitely, on a thumb drive." He spreads his hands. "There's tons of malware for sale if you know where to look."

"Great, Marshal. So, give me a ballpark figure. How much will it cost?"

I'm bracing myself for bad news—I have very little access to money—when Marshal, his expression quizzical, reaches out to squeeze my breast.

CHAPTER SIX
TINA

When you're a little kid, grownups can do anything they want to you. Anything. My daddy told me that's the law. Grownups can do anything they want to you, no matter how much it hurts.

CHAPTER SEVEN
KIRK

I watch myself react, watch my right-hand curl into a fist, watch the fist slam into Marshal's left eye, watch Marshal jerk backward as I reach into the pocket of my sweats to grasp the handle of a paring knife. The knife has an ultra-sharp ceramic blade shielded by a plastic sheath. Because I've practiced the move, I know that if I press the sheath against my thigh, the blade will slide free.

It doesn't come to that. Marshal covers his eye with his hand, then sinks into his chair. "Fuck, dude, you couldn't maybe say, 'Keep your hands to yourself?'"

That's exactly what the others would demand, all of them. But Victoria and the bunch? They're women. I'm not.

"Keep your hands to yourself," I finally say. "Please."

Marshal looks at me for a moment, then shakes his head. Lesson learned, he's not gonna fight. I offer my fist and say, "No hard feelin's, man. It's just . . . well, you caught me by surprise and I reacted."

He taps my fist with his, relieved, I think, to find the dramatics over and done with. "So, what's this guy. . . ."

"Halberstam."

"Yeah, what's Halberstam up to that you wanna take this risk?"

I have to think about it for a moment, to organize my thoughts. "Look, if you reviewed a transcript of one of Halberstam's sessions, you wouldn't find anything to complain about. It'd all seem normal. But the jerk reminds us at every session, and usually more than once, that he holds. . . ." I'm about to say *our*, but catch myself at the last minute. "That he holds Carolyn Grand's future in his hands. If he snaps his fingers, she'll find herself confined to a crazy house for an indefinite period of time. So, maybe I'm completely wrong. Maybe Halberstam's on the up and up. Maybe he sincerely wants to help me. But I've dealt with malignant therapists before and I'm not willing to take the chance."

"I hear that, Kirk, and I can't criticize you." Marshal nods agreement. "But I can't give you a price off the top of my head. Like what you want's not somethin' I do, so I gotta look around. Give me a day."

Back in our dark apartment, I strip off my sweats and slide into bed, still nobody else awake. The bed feels empty tonight, empty and enormous, with me a tiny speck barely afloat in an empty ocean.

I'm still keyed up and I draw my legs toward my chest. For all the macho bullshit with Marshal, at heart I'm scared shitless. I'm scared and I'm tired of living under threat and I'm thinking maybe we weren't meant to survive. I mean, not every baby lives to be an adult. Thousands and thousands of little kids die every year. And not just from disease or accident. Maybe we were meant to be one of them.

All in a rush, Hank Grand—I won't call him our father—leaps into my consciousness. He's been lingering, a shadow just out of sight, and now he's come to say hello. Unlike the rest, I watched the movies, as much as I could stand. Hank appeared in many, his blurred face no more than a dancing gray balloon. I was also shown a mug shot taken when Hank was first arrested. His regular features were composed, his mud-brown eyes slick and shiny, his posture relaxed. Like he didn't give a shit.

I picture those zombie eyes, compare them to Halberstam's. The doctor's blue eyes glittered with life, with . . .

The bed shrinks as a question forms. Halberstam's eyes are first of all calculating. For him, it's about making plans, devising strategies, putting them into play. It's about watching other people dance to his tune. But there's need there, too. Need and lust.

So, which of the two—Hank Grand or Laurence Halberstam—is more dangerous? Or are the threats merely different, neither one more or less deadly than the other?

Suddenly I feel Eleni's presence, as real as if she were breathing in my ear. As if she were spooned into me, holding me in her arms. Victoria and Martha have been dominating the body for almost two weeks, leaving Eleni, Serena, and me to communicate in bits and pieces. Halberstam's been the sole topic most of the time, specifically whether Eleni should let him into her pants. That's not Eleni's style, not at all, but the way we're thinking, Halberstam won't commit us as long as he gets laid every so often.

Lying here now, thinking about Halberstam's cold stare, I've had a change of heart. Halberstam doesn't need an incentive to keep us around. He'll toy with us until he decides we're no longer fun. And then—

I stir, suddenly restless, when Tina's voice sounds in my ear. "Daddy," she announces, her tiny voice surprisingly cool, "will come for me. Daddy always comes for me."

CHAPTER EIGHT
SERENA

I don't find il Dottore's office bland, only soothing, colors not a single shade as Victoria claimed. Pale threads of orange and red and ochre and green running through the fabric of the wallpaper, the blue edge of a robe worn by a porcelain statue of the virgin in a lit niche, a celadon bud vase, a dragon of lavender jade that belongs in a museum, two rosy-red pigs on their hind legs doffing top hats, they lead my eyes around the room, from pleasure to pleasure, the whole screaming money, money, money. The price adds to the seamless whole, everything connected, a single message conveyed in a sensual dance, the chefs' cliché confirmed: you eat first with your eyes.

Il Dottore's working hard when I enter his sanctuary, the picture of diligence, one hand brushing his forehead, leaning forward, shoulders stiff and bent, the posture by now as predictable as it is studied and I know he can't help himself. It's all he's got.

I wait patiently, my delight in the room sufficient for the time being, wait for his gaze to turn my way, wondering if

I'll find the piercing glare reported by Victoria or the predatory calculation discovered by Martha or the lust Kirk recognized. But I don't see any of that when he looks up, only a tired man approaching middle age, hoping against hope to maintain the superhero fantasies that fueled his adolescence. His eyes travel the length of my body, across my windblown hair, amber eye shadow, curving lashes, violet lipstick, over a multitiered necklace of glass beads, my necklace of many colors, a female echo of Joseph's coat that drops into the neckline of a silky white blouse.

"Please introduce yourself," he demands.

"Serena Grand, at your service."

"Ah, you're the one Martha called a troublemaker. Last week, according to Martha, your control of Carolyn Grand caused her to be late for her appointment."

Il Dottore's stilted tone is unexpected, the man trying too hard, his effort only revealing the child beneath, vulnerable, unprotected. I want to console him despite Martha's warning: Do you remember what it was like in the hospital? Don't give the bastard an excuse.

I do remember what it was like, the lost days, weeks, months, heavily drugged, each moment weighing down the next. Cinderblock walls framed the long corridors, every hallway identical. You were in the same place no matter where you were, and the worst part—the absolute worst—your suffering might never end, no time limit to the dead time, no life or liberty or pursuit of happiness. Your most basic rights taken away because you happen to be who you are.

"I did," I admit, my tone contrite. "I was carried away."

"By what?"

"By a chance to exist, to become flesh and dwell among you."

Halberstam responds with a sagacious nod. "'Dwell among you,'" he says. "Very nice. But Carolyn Grand committed herself to an appointment she couldn't keep. And before you say anything about there being no Carolyn Grand, please understand this. From my point of view, there must be a Carolyn Grand, a responsible adult who can function, with appropriate support, in the community."

I can see why Martha hates this man who doesn't get it, who will never understand because he cannot step far enough away from his own needs to know the needs of another, to make those needs his own, a burden freely held.

Victoria whispers in my ear and I repeat what she tells me, word for word. "We've been living at the same address for the past nine years. We have no debts and we never, before the incident, had any contact with the police. In addition, we're good to our neighbors, maintain our apartment and take out the garbage before it begins to stink. As for being a responsible adult? We receive a disability check every month for a good reason. We're disabled."

Halberstam's chin rises as I go on, a thin smile exposing just the tips of his teeth. "Those are not your words, Serena. Whose are they?"

"They belong to Victoria, whose special skill lies in arranging simple ideas in little choppy elements that sound like accusations. But we don't think we did anything to merit commitment, none of us. It's not right."

"I'm afraid right and wrong don't apply to what we're doing. Strictly speaking. But I'm glad you're being honest." He reaches for a fountain pen lying on his desk, picks it up, the better to display the green enameled barrel. "Victoria's presence is a piece of good luck. I can at least be certain that I'll reach a pair of responsible ears." He pauses, takes a breath. "Two things. First, I'm reducing your appointment schedule to three times per week, Mondays, Wednesdays, and Fridays. Second, your father will be released from prison three days from now. He'll be living in a Bronx shelter and subject to close scrutiny, but he's on his own during the day until he finds a job."

I don't respond because there's nothing to say. Here he comes, ready or not.

"As a condition of parole," Halberstam continues, "a court will issue an order of protection forbidding any contact with you. And let me add that your father is sixty-seven years old and has been in one or another sex-offender treatment program for the past five years."

I try to sit up straight, but the chair resists. Still, I manage a smile, Victoria's voice again sounding in my ears. "I sense a warning, Doctor. Despite the reassurances, I sense that you're trying to warn us."

"There's that, too," he finally admits. "I have a hotline number you're to call if he does show up. Will you use it? That's my dilemma in a nutshell. No matter what you tell me, I can't be sure that you won't put yourself in harm's way."

The red light on Halberstam's intercom blinks: on-off, on-off, on-off. He lifts a receiver to his ear and listens for a moment before hanging up. I watch him rise, fingertips still on the desk as he leans forward.

"My apologies. I have an emergency here. You'll have to give me a few minutes."

CHAPTER NINE

KIRK

I'm up and out of the chair, crossing the room, as soon as the door closes. I'm scared, no bullshit about it, but I'm following Marshal's simple instructions. I find a USB port on Halberstam's computer, take a flash drive from Serena's oversized purse, then plug the flash drive into the open port and move to the keyboard. Halberstam's computer has a Windows operating system, and I'm easily able to access the device manager on the control panel, isolate my flash drive and order it to open a program. The download takes less than ten seconds.

I'm back in my seat and trying to relax while Serena demands the return of our body. Nothing to worry about there. I'll be off as soon as Halberstam returns. Satisfied, really fucking satisfied. That's because tonight, at 3:00 a.m., Halberstam's computer will copy its files into one of Marshal's computers. Everything.

I tune Serena out, Victoria, too. Victoria's really pissed at me because I paid for the malware with money from the family till. Tough shit because we can't wait until we're committed, until the locked doors on our locked ward close behind us. That's for suckers and we've been suckers long enough. We need to get out ahead of this prick, to put him in a box.

Halberstam's taking his time and my thoughts finally turn to Hank Grand, a man with even less conscience than Halberstam. They should have killed him; even Serena agrees. Instead, New York incarcerated him at the cost of $60,000 per year and now he'll be walking the streets. Five years of therapy? Plenty of time to get it right, to practice delivering the words asshole therapists want to hear. We know this because we've done it ourselves, learned to mouth the words this or that doctor found comforting.

Yeah, we can let this one go. She's safe.

CHAPTER TEN
SERENA

"I apologize for the interruption, Serena." Halberstam crosses the room and slides onto his chair, his gait surprisingly graceful. "We were discussing your father's release. If there's anything—"

"There is, actually. We want to know why he was freed before the end of his sentence."

Halberstam looks at me for a moment, a question lingering in the arch of his brow, as visible as if spelled out in boldface alongside a cartoon character's head. Is the question impertinent, a gauntlet thrown before his feet?

"I don't work for the Department of Corrections, Serena, nor do I sit on the parole board, but I've spoken to your father's parole officer. As he explained, felons in New York State automatically have their sentences reduced if they behave and your father's behaved for the most part. As a result, his sentence was reduced from thirty to twenty-eight years."

"Doesn't that mean he still has a year to serve? Doesn't that mean our father could still be in prison, where he belongs?"

Halberstam sighs. I'm being tedious. "If your father serves his full sentence, he'll be released without supervision a year from now. As it is, he can be arrested immediately if he violates the conditions of his parole, which include approaching his daughter. You'll be granted an order of protection, by the way, so you won't have to solely rely on his parole officer."

Martha yells at customer service reps, calls them morons, idiots, accuses them of having, collectively, the IQ of a retarded frog. I hear something of that in Halberstam's tone, the exasperation, a frustrated adult coping with a slow child who asks too many questions. I can't fault him because the central fact never changes. Hank Grand is going to be released, and there's nothing he or I can do about it.

Tina's already suffering, the old memories churning up, lava from the heart of the Earth, all consuming, her only sustenance.

"You're drifting, Serena."

"I have nothing to add, Doctor."

"Why not?"

"Because the die, being cast, still rolls, the numbers tumbling over themselves. Wait and see."

"Well put. Now, in my conversations with Victoria and Martha the subject of function came up several times. Martha maintains the household. Victoria is Carolyn Grand's public face. Two others I haven't met also appear to have set functions. Eleni's tasked with satisfying Carolyn's sexual needs. Tina remembers so that the others can forget or at least claim not to have known in the first place. So Serena, and please take your time, describe your function. Tell me what you bring to the table."

I slide my hands between my knees, suddenly shy, this monster man demanding secrets that ordinary humans are allowed to hold close. Others have waited until we were ready to share, until we trusted them, but there's no time here with the court's demands looming. Only a few days from the day of decision, il Dottore's recommending that we continue in therapy, that we remain on the tightrope indefinitely because there's only one alternative—confinement—and we wouldn't want that. Would we?

I'm born ten years ago, when our body is in its twenty-fifth year, my siblings and I floundering, as always, especially Tina after days and days of remembering. The darkness is so intense we can barely move through it, every chore becoming an insurmountable obstacle, the sink full of dishes, the bedroom floor heaped with dirty clothes, the bathroom smelling of piss. And all of us thinking this is it, this time she'll succeed, this time she'll kill us.

Escape the only option, I fly, newborn, through the door and into the street, putting time and space between our body and Tina, my instinct protective, let her rest, let her fall into the oblivion between animations. I walk straight up Flatbush Avenue, lost in the cacophony, a baby learning the difference between reality and memory for the first time. I knew there would be people, cars, and trucks, knew there would be lights and stores, horns and sirens, but I can't sort them properly, can't bring them to scale, sound overlying sound, image overlying image, and what I should simply know I have to construct from the memory of others.

As I pass finally beneath the great arch at Grand Army Plaza, sculptured soldiers above and on both sides, I feel like a foreigner, an alien, the wars of America someone else's history, not ours. And then I'm in Prospect Park and I begin to run though not a fugitive, though unpursued. The late June day is warm and I'm slick with sweat, my body making itself felt, skin and bone, nerve and muscle, taste and touch and smell and sight, my breath running ragged in my lungs, my thighs on fire, half-blinded by the sweat dripping from my brow, at last alive.

I finally turn off the path and stumble down a hill onto a large meadow, others there ahead of me on blankets, scattered about like offerings left for a ravenous god. I fall to my knees, reserves spent, and roll onto my back, patiently waiting for my breathing to calm, for the pulse in my head to fade away, until I can sense the blades of grass against the back of my neck, until clouds and blue sky move apart and I feel a yearning so deep I cannot turn my eyes away. I raise my arms, palms open, reaching upward beyond the illusion of a flat and solid sky—searching, searching, searching—my heart craving the one who truly comprehends the folly of words. Instead I feel yearning in every particle, every galaxy, every solar system, to stop the momentum, to shrink down, eon by eon, to draw closer and closer, now touching, now smiles everywhere.

Call it what you want. Call it Jesus, Buddha, Allah, Zeus, Hera, Parvati, Lakshmi, Amaterasu. Call it Chango, Elegua,

Ogun, Yemaya. Call it the creator who endowed us with certain unalienable rights. It hardly matters because the yearning runs both ways and I know my creator is as helpless as the specks of dust lying out in the meadow. I arch my back, lift my head, reaching up, until my something looks back for a time too short to measure, and my brain whispers: alright, alright, alright.

I don't speak a word of this to il Dottore, not a syllable, not a whisper, my posture at all times submissive, the flower child at night, her petals folded. "Color," I tell him. "My job is to supply color." From a distance, I hear Victoria applaud.

"And do you succeed?"

"Of course. The gray of our lives is sequential, flowing from light to dark, so that a single yellow rose in the center is a thousand yellow roses, enough to light a room."

Halberstam nods, his dismissal apparent, I'm the obvious nutcase described by Martha when I made her late for her appointment, a self rarely in control of the body, a self on the way out, don't let the door hit you in the ass. He takes me through the abuse routine—do I remember—knowing that my response will only be more of the same. The body had been around for more than two decades before my appearance. That job belongs to Tina.

"And will I see Tina soon?"

I want to say only the shadow knows, but I remember Victoria telling me in the plainest language not to get in il Dottore's face, the man believing that patients should always be told, should never tell. He's bored with me besides, the real stars absent—Tina, Eleni—and won't they have stories to share. I finally note the lust in il Dottore's gaze, his flat blue eyes now sparkling.

Ten minutes later I'm on a sidewalk in Midtown Manhattan, still in control, a big surprise because I can feel Victoria's breath in my ear, a sure sign my time on Earth is almost over, at least for now. But Victoria's whispering: "You did good, honey child. You told him exactly nothing. You didn't give him a single excuse."

It comes to me in a flash, the revelation: my sister loves me, loves us all, even Eleni, even those she's marked for elimination, for death, because love doesn't matter here, only survival. Victoria wants to survive, Martha, too, their combined will to live, no matter how bleak the conditions, far more powerful than my own.

CHAPTER ELEVEN
MARTHA

I give the elevator button a nudge on my way to the stairs. I'm not expecting much because the elevator's been down for a week. No biggie. The elevator's broken about half the time and we're used to the stairs. Not this time, though. The blue light above the call button flickers and I hear the elevator descend from somewhere above. It bangs against the housing, a hollow boom that echoes in the hallway.

The elevator door slides back a few seconds later to reveal Roberta, whose last name I don't know. Roberta's a black woman well into her seventies. She's been living here longer than any other resident and she knows everyone. I watch her move into a corner when the door opens, pulling her shopping cart along. I've also brought my shopping cart, which I wedge against the back of the elevator. Then I ride down with my butt against the door.

In New York, food stamp grants are posted to an account accessed through your Medicaid card. That transforms Medicaid cards into temporary credit cards, dispensing dollars until your allotment runs out. Which it always does. Making the day your card refills a spontaneous holiday.

Some people spread their stamps out over the month, but I'm a splurger. I like to fill the shelves, the refrigerator, the tiny freezer. Never mind that two weeks from now I'll be cursing myself because there's no money. I just need to see the cupboards full. I need abundance, no matter how temporary.

"Hey, Carolyn, how you doin'?" Roberta says. "You off to C-Town?"

"Uh-uh, Pathmark." It's mere coincidence that our cards are filled on the same day, but we meet fairly often to discuss what's on sale. Mostly, I look forward to Roberta's company, though I prefer to do the actual shopping alone. I like to weigh every purchase, to calculate and recalculate. One hundred dollars to last a month. Every gram counts.

"Woman come by askin' about you." Roberta's tone is neutral, her eyes turned away. "Name of Porter. Wanted to know if y'all was trouble, makin' noise, confrontin' your neighbors. Wanted to know if y'all have a lot of visitors."

I nod, but I'm too humiliated to say anything. Roberta's not familiar with the others because I do all the shopping. But she knows something's wrong when a healthy, childless woman receives food stamps.

"I told that Ms. Porter, 'Lady, if this is all you got to do, find another job for yourself and save honest taxpayers the cost of your pension.'"

"What did she say?"

"Nothin', just laughed fit to burst." Roberta smiles. "Now there's a woman don't take a bluff."

* * *

We linger in front of the building for a few minutes. Discussing what items are on sale in which stores. Roberta's face is a mass of wrinkles. Her bony frame leans to the left, the result of a small stroke. I watch her finally move away, using her shopping cart for a walker, her left leg dragging. The odds are stacked against Roberta. She's an old woman, poor all her life, her kids far away. But she keeps going no matter what life throws at her. Like us.

I finally head off in the opposite direction. We're into August now, with the temperature at ten o'clock already above eighty degrees. I'm sweating before I reach the end of the block. But I don't mind. With no air conditioner, we're used to sweating out the summer months. Still, it's a relief when I step into the air-conditioned Pathmark on Atlantic Avenue. I stop near the entrance for a moment as the sweat evaporates. To my left, I see Crespo, the manager. Crespo sometimes flirts with me, but he's wasting his time. If I have eyes for anyone, it's Violetta, who works a cash register.

Today I have eyes only for the chuck roast, which is on sale, $3.25 a pound. With just a few cheap ingredients, you can turn a chuck roast into a pot roast good for a lunch and four dinners. I buy two, four pounds each, $25 in total, a quarter of my stamps. As a general rule, I don't measure my shopping by time, thirty days until new stamps come through. I measure the month in meals, ninety-three meals in July to be exact. I know I can't make a hundred dollars produce ninety-three meals, but I can turn a whole chicken into three dinners and four lunches by making chicken stock from the carcass and adding a little rice. Brown rice is a Grand household staple. I buy it in twenty-five-pound bags at a wholesale grocery for about $20. In an emergency, a cup of rice fried up with some onion, peppers, and garlic will pass for lunch. Add an egg, you've got dinner.

I take a certain satisfaction from my skill at making do. Even though I have no idea who will eat the dinner.

I wander into the produce section. In truth, except for basics like onions and carrots and celery, we can't afford fresh fruit or vegetables on the first go-round. Instead, I try to set a few dollars aside from our disability check to buy produce from the city's many sidewalk vendors, a bag of cherries, a head of cabbage or broccoli, a few peaches. The produce is cheaper and fresher.

I'm completely absorbed, turning over bags of carrots, looking for any sign of rot, when I happen to glance up and see my father at the other end of the produce aisle. Instantly, the lie we've been telling each other all these years—the one about only Tina having to relive the past—falls away. My bowels contract, every organ quivering, and I feel an enormous pressure on my chest. For a very long moment, my lungs are completely paralyzed. Nothing has been lost, nothing. The memories, the images swirl around me, circling faster and faster as the words repeat.

To a child, to a child, to a child . . .

CHAPTER TWELVE
ELENI

The body is in full panic mode when I come aboard. Serena, Victoria, and Martha have fled and Kirk is nowhere to be found. That leaves me or Tina to face the emergency and it ain't gonna be Tina. Still, they've picked the right sibling. Although terrible images continue to shred what little mind I possess, I force my brain to calm. I've been in tough situations before. That's what I tell myself. I've been in tough situations and I'm still around and you can kiss my ass.

Besides, who's to say it's Hank Grand? Like Kirk, I've seen the mug shot taken when our father was arrested. He was forty at the time. Now he's sixty-seven.

I study the man on the other side of the store. He's standing before a display of refrigerated jars, probably salad dressing. I can see the resemblance, but I also find differences. In the mug shot, Hank Grand had a full head of hair, but this man's nearly white hair is receding front to back. He's sporting a gut, too, whereas the Hank Grand on those movies was trim. The nose is softer as well, and the jowls entirely new.

I watch him take a jar from the shelf, watch him spin it in his hand as he examines it. The gesture is so casual that

I'm unprepared when he looks up, his head slowly turning until his dead eyes meet mine. I'm expecting to find pure malevolence but instead discover calculation, the look of a man weighing his options. I reach into Martha's purse and wrap my fingers around a canister of mace given to me by a cop who didn't say no. The canister reassures me to an extent, but it doesn't tell me what to do.

From somewhere off in the distance, I hear Tina whisper, "Daddy's come to get me. Daddy always comes to get me."

I've never had all that much patience with Tina. Maybe she mopes for all of us, but she still mopes. Me, I want to live. I don't want to be a mope or a prune, either. Indecision doesn't become me.

Okay, it's time to confront, time to look the bastard in the eye, to gauge his intentions, to measure the threat. After all, the man's on parole. If he admits to being Hank Grand, he can be arrested. According to our lawyer, parole violators are not eligible for bail. Hank would remain behind bars until he receives a hearing that won't take place for six to eight months. Even better, if the scumbag's charged with violating an order of protection, years can tacked on to his original sentence.

"Oh, hey, Carolyn."

The voice comes from behind me. It belongs to a creep whose name badge reads Crespo. He's smiling what he imagines to be a seductive smile.

"What do you want?" I demand.

He draws back, offended. Tough shit. "I just wanted to tell you that we're having a flash sale on tuna fish."

I shake my head and mutter, "Jesus Christ."

"Hey, sorry."

Crespo's eyes widen as he raises a hand and backs off. Good riddance, but when I return to Hank Grand, I find him gone.

Now what? I'm standing in a supermarket, leaning over a shopping cart loaded with groceries, wearing a hideous housedress, my sweat-soaked hair pinned to the side of my head like a fucking helmet. I hear voices, Martha and Victoria rapidly approaching. They want the body returned to their care, but I'm not ready for exile.

"Get your cowardly asses back where they came from," I tell them.

I'm shocked when they quickly retreat, leaving me to a shopping cart loaded with groceries. My first instinct is to abandon the cart where it is and head off. I haven't been out of the apartment in weeks and playing housewife is not on my agenda. But I have to go home anyway, what with the dress and the hairdo. Plus, when you get right down to it, the body has to eat. It's my body, too.

I check out, using the dollars in Martha's wallet to pay for an eight-pack of generic paper towels and two bars of soap. The rest, $67.80, comes off our food stamp allowance. Outside, I cross to the shaded side of the street before heading home. The sidewalks are almost deserted, what with the heat and the humidity, but I'm still scanning the pedestrians—mostly male but occasionally female—for suitability. That said, I'm not the "drug-fueled" nymphomaniac described by my dear sister.

If there's to be a sexual life for us—the way there is for everyone else in this world—the sex will always be casual. It's either that or cross your legs and try to forget. And that's because a true relationship between caring human beings is a nonstarter. No man would put up with the identities rotating through Carolyn Grand's body. Or woman, for that matter.

Maybe two months ago, I met a banker named Mario Spaulding at a club in Lower Manhattan. I was sitting by the bar when he asked me to dance and I said yes without thinking too much about it. Mario wasn't a great dancer, wasn't beautiful, wasn't a hard-body athlete. But something in his manner convinced me that he not only knew where he wanted to go, he knew he couldn't get there unless I came along with him. Partners in crime, both vital to pulling off the job.

The club was on the first floor of a hotel and Mario, a native New Yorker, already had a room. I teased him about his arrogance on the way to the elevator. He refused to deny the charge, but when the door closed on an empty car, he took me in his arms and I felt his erection pushing into my belly. I was thrilled. No performance anxiety tonight. Right to work.

Upstairs, Mario was in no hurry. Me, either. We played with each other's bodies, fingers, hands, mouths, and tongues, until I couldn't bear it for another second. I fell onto my back and he slid inside me, taking his time, moving oh so slowly, filling me, pulling back to the very edge. I reached up, took him by the shoulders, and drew him down so that our chests and bellies met. Smiling, he wrapped an arm around my back, pulled me tighter against him, then leaned down and kissed me, our mouths forming an instant partnership. After a very short time, without Mario speeding up, I came so hard my toes were still curled five minutes later.

We went at it all night. Sex, food, drink, sex, food, drink, talk, talk, talk. I found myself really liking the guy, body and soul. I wasn't a conquest. I wasn't to be dismissed, as I'd been many times before. Our talk was light and teasing, full of promise, of exploration. It continued until shortly before dawn when Mario asked for my phone number. As I kissed him and said goodbye, I rattled off the first set of numbers to cross my mind. I only remember they began with 212.

Imagine Mario trying to call me at our real number. Who would answer? Would they know of his existence? Even the simplest connection—let's get together next week at the same place—doesn't work for a woman with restricted access to her own body.

Nope. Gals like Eleni Grand, we gotta take our lovin' whenever and wherever. But not, as the prunes insist, however.

I listen to the squeaking wheels on the cart as I make my way home, but I'm thinking of my father. It's pretty obvious that his appearance wasn't some kind of coincidence. He must have followed Martha and that means he knows where we live. So, what next? I hear Martha now, very distinctly. There's a Post-it note attached to the refrigerator, she explains, with the phone number of a hotline written across the face. If I would be so good as to relinquish the body, she will use that number to report Hank Grand's appearance. The relinquishing part isn't going to happen. I waited too long to get here. Besides, there's something else that needs doing. The files Marshal hacked are yet to be read because Kirk is being denied any active time.

I don't know how to fight for Kirk. I'm only sure that if the prunes succeed, if they banish him, Serena will be the next to go. Then me.

I take the meat out of the shopping cart as soon as I get into the apartment. I put it in the refrigerator but leave everything else. I can't help but notice the Post-it note with the phone number written in red ink. On impulse, I punch the number into our landline. I'm expecting some kind of breathless response. It's a hotline after all. Instead, I reach a man who identifies himself as Detective Phil Wocek. I explain the situation as best I can, Hank Grand out on parole, the order of protection, the conditions of parole. Wocek maintains complete silence—I'm not even sure he's still there—until I finish.

"Okay, lemme check it out," he says.

For the next ten minutes, I listen to the faint chatter of a police radio and the voice of a desperate-sounding man who keeps shouting, "No, no, no."

Finally, the phone's picked up. "Sorry for the delay," Wocek announces. "But it looks like your order of protection hasn't been processed yet."

"My father's release has been in the works for months. But what? The judge couldn't get around to it?"

"No need for the sarcasm, Ms. Grand." The cop's tone has all the passion of a computer-generated voice on a corporate phone menu. "We're paddlin' as fast as we can."

I take a breath. "He still violated his parole. Why don't you call his parole officer?"

"As a matter of fact, that's exactly what I'm gonna do. But I wouldn't expect much. I mean, your father was on the other end of the store when you saw him for the first time in twenty-seven years. He never spoke to you, never even approached you. So, unless he admits to deliberately making contact, he's not gonna get arrested. Period, end of story."

The state has failed us again. How shocking. I hang up and head for the shower. On the way, I double-check the dead-bolt locks on the door, making certain they're engaged. I've got a hot date with the showerhead and I don't care to be interrupted.

As I pull off my clothes, I become more and more aroused, that glow in the darkness making its very specific demands. It's a pure pleasure to strip off the sweaty housedress, to shed bra and panties, to adjust the water temperature, then switch the shower to pulse. I stand beneath the water for a moment, allowing the heavy jets to wash through my hair and across my face before reaching up to lift the showerhead off the hook.

That's when the present drops away.

* * *

I'm little and I'm in a tub and the water is hot, so hot I'm burning and I'm screaming and I can't get out. I can't get out, I can't get out. Daddy holds me down and he's so strong, too strong, please, please, please, and then his voice, his calm, calm voice.

"This is what happens to bad girls, Carolyn. I told you not to be a bad girl. I told you again and again. Now, see what you made me do?"

CHAPTER THIRTEEN
KIRK

When I come alive, our body's on the bathroom floor, sobbing. There's nothing I can do but wait for long minutes until it calms. But that's all the latitude I'm allowing. There's no room for bullshit self-pity, no matter how fucking pitiful we really are. I'm not afraid that Hank Grand will kill us. I'm afraid he won't, that he'll bend us to his will, that he'll eventually break us, that he'll leave us even more fucked up than we already are. If that's possible.

I make my way into our little bedroom, pull on underwear, a pair of loose-fitting jeans and a gray hoodie. Then it's off to the silverware drawer in the kitchen where I retrieve the paring knife I usually carry. It's obvious, by now, that Hank Grand's willing to bide his time, that he's content to study his prey. It's been a long time, and the asshole needs to know who we are before he makes his move.

All to the good, the extra time. I'm a fucking Boy Scout and I intend to be prepared, even if that means cutting the bastard's throat. I head for Marshal's, dragging all our memories with me. Eleni was right. There's no escape. No more hiding behind poor Tina. We *are* Tina.

Marshal has a woman in his apartment when I arrive. Her name is Mary and she has the sort of contented look that follows a serious workout. I'm hoping she made up for me punching him in the eye.

"You here about the material?" Marshal asks.

"Yeah."

"I looked it over and there's something you gotta see." He glances at his girlfriend. "Mary's gonna head home as soon as her ride shows up. We'll take a look after. In the meantime . . ."

There's a half-smoked spliff in a cut-glass ashtray. Marshal gestures to it, but I refuse. Weed can sometimes take you to a whacked-out place, a paranoid place. Which, when I think about it, is pretty much where I'm already at.

"I'm gonna go for walk," I announce, mostly because I can't sit still. "Be back in a half hour. Nice meeting you, Mary."

Outside, I scan the block to the north and south. There's no sign of Hank Grand, but I do get lucky. A woman I don't know approaches, a sudden smile brightening her face. She's an acquaintance, no doubt, of one of my sisters. Me, I've dealt with this situation before and my return smile is even more genuine because she's smoking a cigarette. Martha's budget for the Grand household does not include the price of tobacco.

I chat with the woman—her name is Dorian—for a few minutes. It turns out she works at the library Victoria uses for research. Victoria's been getting a college degree at City University for the past eight years. Taking one course at a time, rarely completing any on schedule. Still, she's close now, or so she claims.

"Listen," I tell Dorian as she's preparing to walk away. "I wonder if you'd be willing to part with a smoke? I've been tryin' to quit, but right about now it's killing me."

"Been there," she says as she reaches into her purse. "Done that."

Dorian's about my age and cute. A pudgy blonde with a quick smile and sharp, intelligent eyes. I'm instantly attracted, but her gaze reveals zero interest. I have to content myself with a quick check of her ass when she strolls away.

I decide to walk around the block, maybe burn off a little energy while I enjoy my rare cigarette. Once I get started, I can't stop. I keep walking, past the trendy cars and the shops on gentrified Fulton Street, then along Lafayette Avenue with its impressive townhouses. My eyes never stop moving and I've made up my mind. If I spot our father, I'm gonna make him admit his identity. I'm gonna make a point as well. We're not nine years old. We're not his defenseless daughter, not anymore. If he fucks with us, we're prepared to resist.

I'm thinking about how close fear is to hate when I knock on Marshal's door fifteen minutes later. I'm thinking either one is motive enough to drive the blade of my knife into Hank Grand's chest.

Inside, Marshal leads me to the spare bedroom that houses his computers, keyboards, and a host of peripheral devices, none of which I can identify. Marshal holds a degree in musical composition from NYU. In his unlimited spare time, he composes electronic music that he shares with online friends. Myself, I'm drawn to grungy rock bands working venues where the women have enough piercings to set off metal detectors a hundred yards away.

"I worked with your shrink's files for hours," Marshal says. "But I got almost nothing. The files are encrypted and I can't find the key. Also, Halberstam's permanently deleting his emails. An expert might be able to recover them. Not me."

I watch him tap the keyboard, watch his computer, a laptop, jump to life. "So, what am I doing here?"

"I found one email in his Sent message box and you need to see it. According to the time stamp, it was written a few hours before his computer dumped its files. It's probably been deleted by now."

"What about his patient files?"

"If you're thinking I can break his encryption, Kirk, I'm more likely to break into Billboard's Top Fifty list."

I smile as I wave him off. "Okay, let's take a look."

Zenia, my dear. Greetings from sweltering New York. On days like today, when it's too hot for my daily run, how I do envy your move to ultra-temperate San Diego. In your part of the world, the average high in August is 76 degrees. In bustling New York, the temp broke 90 this afternoon, as it has for the past four days, cooking the brick, the concrete, and the asphalt in the process. I'm living in an oven.

But there's good news, too. I've acquired a patient, a private patient who I'm able to bill at my full rate. No medical insurance discount, no cut-rate Medicaid reimbursement. The bills are being paid by Patricia's daddy, the same daddy who molested her for years. As the crimes went unreported, Daddy continues to play a central part in her life, although he keeps his hands and his other parts to himself these days. The truth, that he lost interest when she matured, is as obvious as it is unavailable to her. She believes that he's reformed.

Patricia presents just as obviously.

I'm thirty-one years old, and I've weighed more than two hundred pounds since I was sixteen? Daddy came into my room at night.

I have no friends and spend my lonely nights watching reality television? Daddy came into my room at night.

My co-workers hate me, and I only have a job because my father makes them put up with my obnoxious behavior? Daddy came into my room at night.

Zenia, dear, you're familiar, of course, with the underlying principal: don't blame me for anything because I'm not responsible. In our profession, we listen to this blather every day. Patients like Patricia come to us because they're in pain. They tell us they have a right to their pain, but it still hurts. Please take my pain away they demand, without damaging my sense of entitlement.

Under the circumstances, as you taught me so long ago, we'd be fools not to liven the long hours we spend absorbing their self-pity. As for Patricia, I'm going to tell her that salvation depends on her performing a task she cannot possibly perform. I'm going to advise her to lose those hundred pounds.

You also asked after my multiple. No real news on that front. I'm still waiting for the elusive Eleni. But the father has now been released. How I'll use him, if I'm able to use him, remains to be seen. Something interesting, however, did arise in the course of

Carolyn Grand's second visit. I believe I mentioned that Martha was the particular identity on that morning and that she was late. She excused her tardiness by claiming that an identity named Serena "hijacked" the body. How did she know that Serena was the hijacker? Martha knew because she was there, present, but unable to exert any measure of control. I don't have to explain my instinctive skepticism. You know me too well. Two identities present at the same time? Why not three or four? But then I reviewed the literature and it seems this phenomenon has been commonly reported. One identity in full control of the body with others (voyeurs?) along for the ride. Fascinating.

I'm not surprised by any of it. The arrogance or the narcissistic chuckle at the end of every sentence. Halberstam's the creepy asshole Serena took him for. But what I'm not finding is an immediate threat. Halberstam appears to be enjoying his time with us. We're okay for now.

"There's more, a lot more," Marshal says when I return the printout. "I did a little checking online. I mean I don't wanna pry and I definitely would've asked first. Only you didn't come around, and I didn't know if I should talk to—"

"One of the other multis?"

Marshal's grin is apologetic. "Yeah, like that."

I should probably reassure him, but I don't. Multi seems too much like an epithet. Something a mob would hurl at you. "So, you said there's more. Give it up."

"Okay, follow me. What jumps out at you in that email?"

"Halberstam's a creep with power."

"True, but what else?" When I shrug, he adds, "The name, man. C'mon."

"What name?"

"Zenia." He leans forward. "First thing, I checked out one of those websites where they list baby names. Zenia's a Greek name, something to do with Zeus, but it's never been listed among the top ten thousand baby names in the United States."

"Which means exactly what?"

Marshal throws up his hands. He's gone way out of his way to help us and I'm acting as though I were doing him a favor. Nice.

"Go ahead," I tell him. "And I'm sorry. But what with learning that our prick of a therapist thinks his patients are play toys, I'm not in the best of moods."

"Yeah, I get it." Marshal lights the spliff, takes a hit and passes it over. I know he wants me to join him and I do. "Okay, Kirk, what I figured was that Zenia is such an unusual name that I'd be able to find your shrink's Zenia without too much trouble. No such luck. It seems like there's not a single Zenia on the planet famous enough to be included in a Google search."

"Nobody?"

"Right. In fact, the name Zenia is also spelled Xenia, and I found a tennis player named Xenia Knoll. But no Zenias." Marshal takes a second turn on the joint. He offers it to me, but when I shake my head, he drops it into an ashtray and heads off to the kitchen. A minute later, he returns bearing a pint of pistachio ice cream, a dinner plate, two spoons, and a carving knife. He cuts the ice cream container in half, lays the two halves on the plate and passes me a spoon. Being as ice cream's a rare treat for us, I get right to work.

"I wasn't ready to give up," he explains. "And I finally did what I should have done in the first place. I googled Halberstam's name and found his Facebook page. No Zenias there, either, but he listed his degrees, including the doctorate in clinical psychology he earned at the SUNY graduate school in Stony Brook. That was in 1996 when he turned twenty-five."

"You think it's real? The diploma?"

"I know it's real, Kirk, because I checked out the med school's yearbook for 1996 and there he was. Take a look. This was on his yearbook page."

Marshal's grinning now, a proud little-boy's grin as he slides his chair to a nearby computer and starts it up. I watch, impressed by the computer's speed. It takes less than a minute before Marshal raises a dramatic finger and brings it down on a single key. A second later, a photo appears on the monitor.

Maybe twenty years younger, Halberstam's posed in a laboratory alongside three young men and an older woman. Oddly, though it's Halberstam's yearbook page, the woman is in the center. The men stand to either side, with Halberstam all the way to the right.

"She got a name?" I lean forward to read the photo's caption, but the letters are blurred. No biggie. Marshal's printed out the page and blown up the caption. The woman's name is Zenia Burgos, professor of clinical psychology, founder of the Burgos Trauma Resolution Center. Halberstam calls Zenia, in the last sentence, "my guiding light."

"That's it?" I ask.

Once again the satisfied smile. "Nope."

Me, I don't really care about Zenia because I don't see what she has to do with us. But I don't want to mess with Marshal's high, either. I accept the printout he offers: a short article published ten years ago in *Newsday*. On page sixteen.

"I found it on a search for the Burgos Resolution Center," Marshal explains. "It's the only relevant item out there."

The piece is quite short. In 2004, a group of former patients filed a class-action lawsuit accusing the center of malpractice. The lawsuit alleged cult-like practices and patients kept against their will. It also named three defendants: Zenia Burgos, Mathew Ostovsky and Laurence Halberstam.

"The center no longer exists," Marshal tells me. "So, the lawsuit at least had that effect. And it looks like Zenia moved three thousand miles away afterward, so there's that, too. But the case was settled before trial, with the settlement naturally including a nondisclosure agreement. The details never became public."

I thank Marshal for the email and the research, but I'm thinking so what? The review board that hired Halberstam has faith in his professional abilities, which is all that matters. Still, it's good to know what we're up against. Even if it means confirming our worst fears.

"Anything else, Marshal?"

"Not really. Halberstam's Facebook page is mostly about his specialty, treating victims of childhood trauma. You cannot go forward until you confront your past. That seems to be his mantra.

CHAPTER FOURTEEN
VICTORIA

For once, I'm not forced to watch Halberstam bent over his notes while I cool my heels in the submissive chair at the start of our session. That's because he's not in the room. As you'd expect, I'm drawn to his desk and our files, my object to know, finally, his plans for our future. Such is the nature of power, such is the fear power generates, and I take a tentative, compulsive step before I stop myself. If he should walk into the room . . .

No desk, that much is obvious, and I construct a nightmare hypothetical, our freedom hanging in the balance, my compulsive curiosity tipping the scales. Who's got the straitjacket?

Nevertheless, I do wander from niche to niche inspecting his precious objects. Most of the small objects in the niches are new, drawn apparently from a larger collection. My little pigs with their top hats have been replaced with a porcelain flask, yellow with delicate blue flowers rising on winding stems. The lavender dragon, my favorite, has been replaced by a lacquered box. A golden carp swims across its black lid, the fish so perfectly executed it appears to be in motion.

I hear the door open and turn to face Dr. Halberstam. His eyes move across my body, but there's nothing prurient in his examination. Halberstam's gotten fairly good at identifying us before we reveal our names. He's obviously proud of this accomplishment, but it's happened with every therapist who stuck with us for more than a month. I'm wearing tan slacks and a thin white blouse, thinner than I like but a necessity given the heat radiating from the sidewalks. My makeup is minimal, my hair swept along the side of my head and fastened with a dark blue barrette.

"Serena," he says at last.

"Sorry, try again."

"Oh, yes, the dowdy outfit. I should have known. You're Victoria."

"Correct."

"Please." Halberstam gestures toward the submissive chair and I dutifully follow his command, surrendering to gravity. I'm thinking about the email Marshal discovered, a copy of which I found on our dining table. Our therapist's a man who likes to play with other people's pain, but there's nothing we can do about it. Hacking is a crime, a felony in New York and—

"We've been working together for how long?" Halberstam's voice jerks me to attention. "Six weeks now?"

"About that."

"So, we're talking about more than twenty-five visits."

I know where this is going and it's not to a place I want to visit. I know also that I have no choice. Halberstam is a predator wise enough to foreclose all lines of retreat. We know him now, except for Tina who's been gone so long I half expect her to never return.

"I haven't been counting, but that seems right," I say.

"Do you see the problem?"

I'm tempted to say, "Yes master." But I'm not Eleni and I don't. "You want to meet Eleni and Tina."

"I can fully understand Tina's reluctance, assuming she is, as you say, the only one who remembers."

"That's changed now."

"Changed?"

"Since my father stepped into our lives. We remember." I somehow manage to maintain a reasonably flat tone, though I'm shaking inside. The flashbacks rip into me without warning. Maybe, at some point, I'll be able to knit them into a whole, a coherent past. Not yet.

I watch Halberstam open the center drawer of his desk and remove a fountain pen, his favorite prop. He stares at it for a moment, then says, "Well, that's something we need to talk about. Later, perhaps. For now, let's discuss the report generated by Adult Protective Services. Some of your neighbors have complained about you, Victoria, and the landlord claims that you're uncooperative and often late with the rent."

On another day, I might be upset. Not today. Ms. Portman has already called us. As far as APS is concerned, we're functioning adequately, a conclusion they've reported not to our therapist but to the court. As for our dear landlord, Muhammad Nazari, he wants us out, so he can raise the rent on our rent-stabilized apartment by 20 percent. Thus, he harasses Carolyn Grand, as he harasses all his tenants, as landlords all over this city harass their tenants. According to Ms. Portman, Doyle was the only other person to complain.

"No reaction, Victoria?"

"I can't address nebulous complaints. As for paying the rent, we've always, month after month, for all the years we've resided in the building, paid our rent before the tenth."

Halberstam stares at me for a few seconds, then swivels in his chair as he searches for a more productive line of attack.

"Alright, let's return to our original topic. I've seen Kirk three times, Serena twice, you eight times, and Martha fourteen times. But I've never seen Eleni or Tina. That's very convenient, Victoria. Convenient for you. As for myself, I'm beginning to doubt they exist."

"I don't blame you. Nevertheless—"

"No." Halberstam points the fountain pen, an accusing finger if I've ever seen one, at the center of my forehead. He's become more domineering with every session. "The incident that brought you to the attention of the court? Blamed on a nonexistent identity, it need never be explained. And your brutal past? If you invent an identity in charge of remembering, you need never review it." He leans back in his chair, seemingly content. "Are you playing me, Victoria? Are you hustling me? Do you consider me an inconvenience imposed by the court, an inconvenience you can simply dismiss?"

I remain calm, my legs crossed, my hands in my lap, my expression (I hope) interested, but unimpressed.

Halberstam drops his hand to his desk. "Now, we've spoken about Carolyn's life with her father at some length in the past. Her loyalty to him, though utterly misguided, was only to be expected. But we haven't touched on what happened later, when she was put into foster care with . . ." He pauses to check the file on his desk. "With the Aceveda family. I assume you remember now."

I manage to scoot up on my chair until I'm more or less perched on the edge. That way, as I give Halberstam his cheap thrill, I can lean toward him, share a few confidences. I steel myself against the unavoidable profanities, but when I finally speak, my bitter tone reveals as much as the words themselves.

"With the Acevedas? Carolyn was a whore, Doctor. That's how she thought of herself, how the other girls thought of themselves. Whores, hookers, working gals, and sometimes when they were really feeling ambitious, escorts. But whatever she called herself, at the end of the day, Carolyn did the fucking and her foster parents, that would be Angela and Benny, kept the money. Whore? Pimp? No more than words to Carolyn. The Acevedas took care of their little moneymakers. They fed Carolyn, clothed her, even sent her to school."

"To school? Why didn't she say something? She did eventually let a school counselor know about her father."

"And where did it get her? No." I stop suddenly, as the memories pour into my awareness. Everything I want to forget. "Two things, Doctor. The Acevedas were a step up for Carolyn. And if they never showed the girls any affection, they never punished them, either. And the sex part? At age ten, eleven, twelve, thirteen? Sex was all Carolyn Grand ever knew." I take a moment to let the anger drain away. I have a point to make and I don't want Halberstam to confuse the issue. "It's funny how foster-care boys get all the attention, joining gangs, heading off to prison or dead in the street. You don't hear much about the girls, but certain outcomes are pretty obvious. The boys think violence is the only way up. The baddest get the most. Now ask yourselves what the girls have to offer when they hit puberty and start hanging out. How do they survive? What tools can they deploy? Even if they haven't been molested already."

"And what about Carolyn?" Halberstam's expression doesn't change.

"Carolyn escaped."

"How?"

"She went insane. Our father made sure of that."

"Ah, your father." Halberstam's eyes are bright enough to reveal his excitement. Perhaps that's because he's got one more surprise. "I'm glad you brought him up. His parole officer, Kevin Powell, phoned me earlier. Your father, it seems, wants to . . . reconcile is too grand for his aspirations. He wants to atone."

Inside, I'm begging anyone to take control of the body: Martha, Eleni, Kirk, Serena. The humiliations are too much for me, my dignity too important, and if the others laugh at my pretensions, they're still my pretensions. Everything about me, from my hair to the generous cut of my slacks to my polished shoes with their two-inch heels, every item is meant to establish a dignity we've never believed ourselves entitled to. Dr. Halberstam means to strip that away.

"You need to be more specific. What exactly does *his* atonement require from *us*?"

"A supervised meeting at a neutral site. Where it goes from there is strictly up to you." He brings his hands together, steeples his fingers. "According to Officer Powell, your father is no longer the man you knew. He's spent most of the last twenty-seven years in isolation and the remainder in therapy. Please understand, I'm not necessarily recommending that you accept the offer and we don't have to decide today. Think it over."

His smile curls around his narrow face. Everything in time. Again, I start to rise, and again he stops me with a wave of his hand. "Now, you were six years old when your mother left. Is that right?"

"She ran for her life."

"Leaving you behind." He pauses long enough to allow his point to fix itself in my brain. "But that's another issue we'll save for a later date. For the present, I'd like to hear about your life before she left. Please, whenever you're ready."

I don't want to remember and Halberstam knows that, his eager look giving his game away. And he's right, on one level. We've always hidden behind Tina. With that defense gone . . .

"I only remember the fighting, my mother bleeding, calling for help I couldn't provide. As for Carolyn Grand, I can't be sure because it all happened so long ago, but I think my father mostly ignored his daughter until his wife left him."

"And afterward . . ."

CHAPTER FIFTEEN
TINA

What do you wanna hear first, Doctor? How it feels to be torn in half? How it feels to be chained and whipped in front of a paying audience? Wanna hear how it feels to know that men all over the world download videos of your degradation, that they jerk off to your pain, your suffering, that they do not give a shit? I can tell you, Doctor, because I know every trick in the fucking book, because I live in a hole in hell. So, what do you wanna know? Just tell me, you bastard, and I'll make all your fantasies come true.

CHAPTER SIXTEEN
MARTHA

It's ten o'clock in the morning. I'm ironing clothes, one of my favorite activities, while *Valerie's Home Cooking* plays on our TV. Valerie's dedicated her Food Network show to budget-stretching casseroles, an important part of our nutritional strategy. I'm not paying all that much attention. I'm thinking of Tina and I'm intensely proud. Tina vanished before Halberstam could ask a single question, leaving Victoria to handle the aftermath. But Tina spoke for all of us. Eloquent and fearless.

I know this because Victoria left a note on the table, along with a printout of Halberstam's email. We've come together since Marshal discovered that email, a matter of pure necessity. A reunion with Hank Grand? We're far more likely to kill than kiss him.

Still, I'm feeling good this morning as I bend to the task at hand. We have an extensive wardrobe. No surprise, given the differences between us. As virtually every item was bought at a thrift store, our clothing needs frequent care, and I'm as good with a needle as I am with an iron. Plus, I've got a pork shoulder cooking on the stove, the recipe pulled off a "cooking hints" website. I've long forgotten the name of the site, but the basic concept is so simple and the results so terrific that I've used it dozens of times. Take a cast-iron stockpot, add a dollop of molasses, a tablespoon of sugar, a tablespoon of salt and a two-liter bottle of store-brand cola. Heat the ingredients until they mix, then add your pork butt and simmer until a thick crust forms on the outside. The sweet-and-sour flavor of that crust is as good as any barbeque sauce. As we'll be eating it in one form or another for the next week, it better be.

I pause long enough to draw the odor of the pork through my nose and into my lungs. Pure drudge pheromones. Then I turn back to the ironing board. Unkempt does not fit my self-image and I make sure we at least appear sane. Just now I'm working on one of Eleni's peasant blouses. The blue one with the scoop neckline that scoops way too low for my taste. The blouse has ruffles at the neckline and waist, forcing me to open each fold and test the iron as I go along. The task is complicated by the delicate rayon fabric. Let the iron get too hot and it's bye-bye blouse.

Forty minutes later I'm working on the last item, a pair of slacks worn by Victoria. I'm looking forward to a cup of coffee, my reward for being a good drudge, when the phone rings. We don't get a lot of calls and I check the caller ID before answering: Legal Aid Society. Already, I'm annoyed.

"Hello."

"Good morning," a woman says. "Am I speaking to Carolyn Grand?"

I'm tempted to bust her bureaucratic chops by declaring that Carolyn Grand doesn't exist. I want to tell her that she's talking to a fragment of a theoretical woman. I want to tell her to go fuck herself. Instead, I simply say, "You are."

"This is Malaya Castro. I'm representing you—"

"What happened to Mark Vernon?"

"He's been moved to another division." She waits for a moment, but I have nothing to say. "So, how have you been?"

"Does it matter?"

"Pardon me."

"I'm busy, Ms. Castro."

"It's Mrs. Castro, but you can call me Malaya."

"Fine. Please state your business, Malaya."

I listen to the lawyer breathe into the phone. I know she's wondering what she did to merit the hostility, but I'm not about to explain. Dimly, I sense Victoria's arrival.

"If I promise to deliver good news," Castro says, "will you ease up on the attitude?"

I smile. Attitude is the only public face I have. Take it or leave it. "Okay, Malaya. But I've got a lot to do today."

"So, I just read the report from Adult Protective Services and it's a hundred percent favorable. You've been living on your own for years now, living responsibly and functioning well despite limited resources. According to APS, there's no reason to suppose you won't continue to function if supervision is withdrawn."

"What does that mean? For Carolyn Grand?"

"It means that I intend, with your permission, to immediately petition the court to end supervision."

"Again, what does that mean? How will it change my life?"

"The review will take about three weeks. If it goes your way, you'll simply become autonomous. Free to get on with your life."

Free to get rid of Halberstam is what I'm hearing. As if our dear doctor would allow that to happen. "According to Mark Vernon, the doctors make the final decision. Not the court."

"That's true. They will."

"Then it's up to Dr. Halberstam."

"No, you've got it backward. Your therapist was appointed by a medical review board attached to the court. Halberstam's recommendation will play a large part in their final decision but not the only part." She pauses for a moment, then says, "You seem pretty certain that Dr. Halberstam will recommend against ending supervision? Don't you get along?"

For once I don't say the first thing that jumps into my head, which is that we're as much a plaything for Halberstam as we were for our father. Like any spoiled child, Halberstam won't give up his toy without a fight.

"I've known a lot of therapists over the years, Malaya, and Halberstam's not my favorite, not even close. But that's not what it's about. Halberstam believes my therapy should continue indefinitely. I can't imagine him recommending anything else when he writes his report."

"Carolyn, I'm your lawyer and I've got your back. I'll make it clear, in the petition, that you're satisfied with your progress and that you intend to remain in therapy. Remember, you're on conditional release, the condition being your therapy. We're only asking the court to make your release unconditional. And no, I'm not a prophet, but I think the odds are with you as long as you keep it together for the next few weeks. Think you can do that?"

I almost say "We'll give it our best," only correcting myself at the last second. The last thing I want to do is explain who and what we are. "I'll give it my best."

"Good, because once your release is granted, you can drop Dr. Halberstam if that's what you want. The decision will be yours to make. From our point of view, the only issue is whether or not you can function on your own. In light of the fact that you've been doing exactly that for a decade, the issue resolves itself."

CHAPTER SEVENTEEN
VICTORIA

An online course I once took on the history of New York City described the development of Brooklyn Heights, a promontory overlooking the harbor. The area began with an investment, a purchase of land by a blue blood named Hezekiah Pierrepont. Pierrepont immediately subdivided his property and offered the lots to others of his caste, who snatched them up. That's because the richest New Yorkers desperately wanted to get their families out of town in the summer. Cholera, smallpox, typhus, diphtheria, and yellow fever ran through the crowded streets of Manhattan during the long hot months from the end of June to September. The only protection was distance.

The epidemics are long gone, but not the heat and humidity that gave rise to them. Nobody moves to New York for the climate, and the hum of air conditioners in summer is almost as loud as the traffic on the street. Still, just as the January thaw brings out the multitudes in winter, so do the few pleasant days that turn up every summer. Days like today when the high temperature will barely clear eighty degrees and the sunlight is unbearably clean, when a breeze sensual enough to cool Eleni's overheated libido ruffles the leaves of an oak on the other side of the walkway.

I'm sitting on a bench in crowded Prospect Park, not far from the zoo. The atmosphere is celebratory, every seat occupied. Two women across the way sit behind strollers, identical except for color: one pink, one blue. Their conversation is animated, though in a language I don't recognize, and they laugh frequently. On the other end of my bench, a middle-aged man feeds a trio of gray squirrels from a bag of peanuts. In slacks and a blue shirt ironed well enough to meet Martha's standards, he glances at me from time to time. I'm in a sleeveless dress that drops to the top of my knee, even with my legs crossed.

I'm thinking the man will strike up a conversation, but there's no room in our lives for a close relationship, a fact Eleni complains about from time to time. She chooses to deal with the problem by engaging in the most casual of relationships, ignoring the obvious dangers. That's not my way.

The man disappoints me by simply walking off, crumbling and tossing his peanut bag into a trash basket. Despite my lack of interest, my reaction is thoroughly female when I ask myself a simple question: what's wrong with me? The question is so stupid that I laugh to myself, a laugh that dies abruptly when I see my father sitting on a bench fifty yards away.

Panic, rising in an instant, tears into my core, ignoring flesh and bone, the same fear that tore through Martha in Pathmark, that compelled all of us save Eleni to choose oblivion over confrontation. A shiver rises along my spine, vertebra by vertebra, to rattle finally through the small bones at the back of my neck. More than helpless, I feel already punished, already in pain.

I want to leap to my feet, to flee, but I remain frozen. I tell myself that I'm in a crowded public park and perfectly safe, but I don't believe it. My terror is primitive, the fear of a peasant for the troll who lives under the bridge. The evil is physical, a presence, a hand already gripping my throat.

Time passes: a minute, then two. My father and I sit unmoving, our time stopped. I'm trying hard to become angry, but my rage vanishes, a drop in an ocean named despair. Hank Grand will come for his daughter, no matter the consequences. Even if I took his picture with a cell phone I don't have, even if I proved it was Hank Grand sitting on that bench, it wouldn't matter. Returning him to prison would only postpone our reunion.

What would Eleni do? What would Kirk do? I've trained myself to appear reasonable, to present a face the world is ready to see, a bearable face, almost professional. But I have no face for the beast, no posture, no expression that could possibly deter Hank Grand.

I raise my head as I finally draw a deep breath and again become aware of my fellow citizens going about their ordinary business, so far removed from my world they might have come from Mars. Our mental disorder—and we are, without doubt, disorderly—is considered a psychosis. We're crazy and I'm willing to admit the fact. But the man on the bench isn't a product of our psychosis. He's blood and flesh and bone, and he means us harm.

I hear Eleni's voice, her arrival so sudden I start. "Take the pepper spray in your purse and spray it into his fucking mouth."

I have to bring my hand to my own mouth, the command so funny that I almost laugh. It's funny, first of all, because I lack the courage and Eleni knows it. But the really hilarious part is that Eleni believes that macing Hank Grand will somehow stop him. It won't.

The day ruined, I have only one recourse and that's retreat. I rise and begin to walk north, toward Grand Army Plaza and away from Hank Grand. I tell myself not to look back, a resolve that lasts for all of thirty seconds. My father has also risen. He's following, his pace matching my own.

And so we go, passing beneath the arch at the plaza, then along Flatbush Avenue, six lanes wide and bustling. Hank Grand comes no closer, but the separation is almost as threatening as an approach. I feel myself shrinking, my shoulders hunched, back bent, so that by the time I turn onto Sixth Avenue behind the Barclays Center I'm fighting hard against an urge to run. There's construction here but no stores or apartment houses. As I glance behind me, a construction worker earns my eternal gratitude when he shouts, "*Ay, mami, eres tan hermosa.*" I don't know what that means, but I'm further encouraged by a pair of whistles from two other workers. Harass me, please.

Ten minutes later, I'm in front of the door to my building, sliding my key into the lock, looking back at my father who stands in the shade of a young maple at the end of the street, still the same fifty yards away. I stare at him for a moment, unable to break off, and I see him, suddenly, as an old man. The bags under his eyes, the furrows above his brow, the swollen jowls, the faint man-breasts, the forward thrust of his gut. He seems almost harmless, just another senior counting the years.

Then he raises a hand and the muscles of his upper arms jerk to attention as he flashes a confident smile.

CHAPTER EIGHTEEN
SERENA

I wake up inside our body, no complaints here. Even with the body reeking of last night's sex, I'm not resentful, although Eleni might practice a bit of hygiene, the omission quite deliberate, a taunt thrown at our two sisters, Martha and Victoria, the prunes. I'm not a virgin, Kirk either, and I suspect the prunes wouldn't be virgins either if they could find a way to fall into bed with each other.

A shower awaits, the urgency apparent from the condition of the clothing scattered across the floor. I gather the skirt, the blouse, the panties, only realizing there's no bra as I dump the bundle into the hamper. Then I'm in the shower, soaping, shampooing, raising my face to the oncoming stream, this treasure not to be taken for granted, only given now, use it or lose it. I stay where I am until the water so predictably cools, until it finally runs cold, too cold even for August in New York.

I grab a towel, dry off, slip into a terrycloth robe Eleni long ago lifted from a hotel room, my first stop the windows overlooking South Portland Avenue in the kitchen and living room. This sequence is now to be undertaken many times each day by whomever controls our body: look to the left, look to the right, is he there, waiting, waiting, waiting, immobile as a lizard on a rock? Our fear marks the boundaries of his and our prison, that we're locked inside with Hank Grand, dancing his dance even when he's nowhere to be found, the orchestra playing on without a conductor.

Ritual complete, the god of fear served, I make coffee, our one true luxury, sadly said because Martha buys the cheapest off-brands on the shelf, Eldorado, Pilon, Café Bustelo, whatever we don't need an extravagance by definition.

I finally settle at the little table we use to dine, a plastic circle three feet across, the surface spattered with the memos we now leave for each other, anything unusual, anything we all need to know, a real family at last. Halberstam's email, Victoria's flight from Prospect Park, the lawyer's petition now delivered to the court, Eleni's vain attempt to activate the coldest of cold hotlines. Our order of protection she was told is still in limbo, so sorry, contested by Hank Grand who insists that his daughter prove that he's a threat, so, so sorry.

A note from Victoria: *Halberstam claims that my interaction with Hank Grand in Prospect Park and on the streets of Brooklyn will be reported to our father's parole officer. We have only Halberstam's word for it. Contact our lawyer? Yes? No?*

I get up, restless, as are we all, knowing what we know, that Daddy is coming, the waiting apace with his strategy, until I yearn for the climax, the final act, the closed door, the period at the end of the sentence. The windows beckon, my thighs forcing me forward though I make no decision to rise, I want out of the apartment despite that the weather turned brutally hot again, a bench, perhaps, in Fort Greene Park near the tennis courts where an overhanging elm offers dark, dense shade.

Look to the right, look to the left, off to the kitchen, look to the right, look to the left, no Hank Grand and I'm so unprepared for the knock on our front door I constrict, literally, arms pressed to my sides, eyes jammed shut as if Daddy were already in the room.

"Hey, it's me. It's Marshal."

I almost ask, "Are you alone," but I catch myself at the last second. I like Marshal, admire him for his soft soul, a man who bears no grudge, an outlier unfit for the universal competition.

Marshal looks me over when I usher him in—who the hell am I—his curiosity genuine. And me, I've met Marshal but only briefly and I know he's wishing for Eleni, Kirk a second choice, no-nonsense Martha as a last resort.

"Serena," I want to caress the side of his face, to reassure, but instead cross my arms behind my back. "What can I do for you?"

He continues to evaluate, unafraid, unjudging. We are who we are, passing souls, elusive as the music he writes in the dark bedroom of his tiny apartment. "I intercepted another email," he explains, "from Halberstam. I thought I'd bring it over."

Ah, Zenia, I write to you in the best of moods, though with little time to spare. My multi has drawn her sword. We are joined in battle. She's submitted a petition to the court demanding she be freed of all supervision. After which, of course, she will surely dismiss your correspondent. That's what comes of being thoroughly disagreeable. Me, not her. Nevertheless, I'm far from finished with Carolyn, who's proven stronger than I expected. I mark her as a true survivor and all the more a challenge because her (many times) tested IQ places her in the very superior range.

First question: is her diagnosis, dissociative personality disorder, accurate? There are those in our community who deny the diagnosis entirely. These patients, they contend, influenced by years of therapy (Carolyn Grand has been in and out of therapy for twenty years, long enough for her various "identities" to become aware of each other), create these personas to avoid personal responsibility, even personal responsibility for their own welfare. As for Carolyn, I'm certain her "identities" tell me only what they think I want to hear, hoping to become free not just of Dr. Halberstam, but of all therapy. They are essentially content with who they are, even if who they are includes propositioning strangers in dangerous neighborhoods.

Two mitigating facts. In the literature, multis are almost always female and almost always have a documented history of horrendous abuse. Carolyn Grand checks both of those boxes. Her childhood was almost beyond imagining. I write this as a therapist who's suffered through many a sad, sad story. We all have. And we've all had patients who use their pasts to justify unacceptable behavior in the present. This behavior further isolates them, leaving them more miserable than they already were. Friendless Carolyn Grand is certainly one of these.

But enough of Carolyn Grand. The court, I promise, will not be releasing her anytime soon. As for me, I intend to reveal her dilemma, whether she likes it or not. I am, as you know and as you taught, ever the manipulator, never the manipulated.

Motto of the story: under no circumstances should you draw your sword on a jaded psychologist.

CHAPTER NINETEEN
MARTHA

I've been chosen to confront the adversary. Another example of the family coming together in the face of a threat. We know what's on the line. The danger's now coming from two sides. Daddy and the doctor. Victoria can't get beyond the injustice. Kirk cannot put aside his rage. Serena hasn't the fortitude. Eleni's never learned to restrain her tongue.

So, here I am, sitting across from the always-dour Tanya in Halberstam's waiting room. My appointment should have started ten minutes ago, but Tanya offers no excuse and no apology for the delay. Sit, wait, be patient.

I don't know exactly how it happens, but Tanya turns to me a few minutes later. Her face expressionless, she says, "You may go in now."

I find Halberstam on his feet. Posed before one of his precious objects, the lacquered box with the gold fish. Recently, he's taken to remaining on his feet through much of our appointment, often with his back turned. When he does approach, I associate the posture forced upon me by the tilted chair with fear. I'm find myself leaning away, as if ducking a blow.

I assume the position without being asked. Halberstam ignores me for a minute as he repositions the box. "I want to try a different approach this time, if you don't mind, Martha."

I nod and spread my hands, though he's not looking at me. "I'm all ears."

Halberstam turns to me, his face all the more threatening for its friendly expression. His eyes are crinkled, mouth turned slightly upward.

"Why are you here, Martha? What do you hope to gain from therapy? What does Carolyn Grand hope to gain?"

I'm tempted to say nothing, to throw it in his face. But that wouldn't be true. We do have a goal and that's to dump his ass without getting ourselves committed in the process. Fortunately, when it comes to therapy—and especially bullshit therapists like Halberstam—I'm no virgin. I know exactly what I need to say.

"Two roads, Doctor. No third way. Either integrate the personalities into one, you might say a reconstructed Carolyn Grand, or eliminate those who prevent us from keeping a simple dental appointment."

"Too general, Martha. Specifically, why are you here in this room at this time? Is it merely because the court ordered you into therapy, then hired me to provide it? You've told me that you cannot work because you cannot show up for work every day. Some identity or another inevitably takes control, whereupon you vanish for two or three days, whereupon you're fired. And yet, you've managed to keep all of your appointments with me."

I don't hear a question, but I respond with the company line, the one our Legal Aid lawyer's already told the court. Still, the words ring so hollow I want to cringe.

"We know we need help, Doctor. Without therapy we'll never meet our goal."

"Which is?"

"To have a life, a real life. Like Pinocchio becoming a real boy."

Halberstam retreats to his desk and takes a seat. He fumbles in the center drawer of his desk, but his hand comes out empty.

"Let's explore that for a moment. How do you pay your rent, Martha? Where does the money come from? Specifically?"

One thing about our doctor, he knows where to insert the probe. I'm to be shown the extent of our dependence. But there's no room for a lie here. Halberstam already knows the answer.

"Two hundred dollars comes from our disability check. The rest from a Section Eight voucher."

"And the food you eat?"

"A hundred dollars in food stamps, plus cash from our disability check."

"And the laundry, who pays for the laundry? And the electric bill? And the cable bill. You do have cable, don't you?"

"Basic." Despite my best intentions, I explain, "You can't get any reception with an antenna. Not in that part of Brooklyn. We tried, believe me."

"I'm more interested in who pays for these things. Who pays for your clothing, your haircuts, your toothpaste, your therapy?"

"The government." There, I've said it. I've said what the bastard wants to hear. I've submitted. "The government pays for everything."

"That's correct. At present, Carolyn Grand is a dependent ward of the state. You say that you wish to become independent, but as I speak to you, I see little evidence to support that assertion. Last week, Victoria, who you claim to be a separate, independent identity, launched a tirade directed at me. She accused me of being a voyeur and called me a fucking bastard." His smile, when he pauses, is cold enough to be a sneer. "My apologies, I've got that wrong. It wasn't Victoria who cursed me. It was still another identity, Tina, who I've been waiting weeks to meet, but who vanished in an instant and hasn't been seen since. Convenient, yes? Carolyn Grand propositions an undercover police officer. Carolyn Grand curses her therapist. But Carolyn Grand need never assume responsibility because she doesn't exist. And let me be quick to add that the language Tina used hardly seems that of a cringing nine-year-old, a little mouse. Something's wrong here, very wrong."

I don't argue the point because I agree with him. I was present when Tina went off on Halberstam. Her tirade was on point, every word cutting to the bone. The only problem is that a nine-year-old couldn't have made it.

"Do you find that surprising, Doctor? That Tina's fear should conceal her rage?"

"No, I find it convenient."

If there's something to be said here, I don't know what it is. Besides, the truth is right in front of his face. I'm wearing a pair of cargo shorts, a plain, white T-shirt, black athletic shoes, no socks and no makeup. My hair's pinned close to the side of my head and my legs are unshaved. How likely is it that I proposition strangers on the street? *Male* strangers.

"You say," Halberstam continues, "that you want to work, but you can't. When was the last time you looked for a job?"

"A year ago."

"Did you find one."

"No."

"And why is that?"

"Because Eleni took the body for a long ride." I can't bring myself to supply the details and I conclude with a shake of my head.

"A character in a book I read a few months ago," Halberstam tells me, "described himself as a half-assed Catholic. 'I'm trying,' he said. 'Only not too hard.' That's you. That's Carolyn Grand. Despite everything, you live a comfortable life, a life that allows your body to be taken for long rides, no obligations to be met. The government check is in the mail."

I finally gather a response, this one true. "Yes, some of us are content. Serena is too fragile to work. Eleni is unconcerned with obligations of any kind. Not Kirk, though. And certainly not myself or Victoria."

"Another excuse from an identity that isn't available. It's just too easy, especially for a woman with a tested IQ in the very superior range, a woman more intelligent than ninety-eight percent of the general population. But except for a free ride, what has it gotten you? That's the question I keep asking myself." Halberstam returns to the center drawer of his desk, but this time he's clutching a sheet of paper when his hand emerges. "I spoke to Kevin Powell, your father's parole officer, earlier this morning. Your father admits to seeing you in Prospect Park, but claims he never came within a hundred yards of where you sat. The other part, about following you home, he denies."

My anger boils up, spills over. "Let me ask you a question, Doctor. Do you consider the word of a sadistic pedophile equal to the word of his primary victim? I say primary because there were many others out on the edge."

This time Halberstam's smile is genuine, the delighted smile of a twelve-year-old boy who's just ripped the wings off a butterfly.

"I'm not judging you, Martha. But Victoria, when she recounted the incident, told me that her father did not approach her. True, she said he remained fifty yards away, not a hundred, but the separation was nonetheless substantial. In any event, only Kevin Powell has the power to charge your father with a violation of the terms of his parole. My function, at this point, is to relay information." He raises the sheet of paper and waves it as though claiming a territory. "This letter is from your father. It's addressed to his daughter, Carolyn Grand. Believe me, I've given the matter a lot of thought. I think it's best if I read it aloud."

Carolyn. I wanna call you my darlin', but I know I got no right. Probably, I shouldn't even be writin' this. I don't know what my PO's gonna say when I show it to him. Maybe he'll ship me back to prison, which I deserve anyway, but it's worth the risk. I feel like I won't ever get it right until I make some kinda peace with myself. I know you hate me and you should. You should hate me as much as I hated my own father, who treated me like I did to you.

I never had much education, comin' here from Missouri after I run away, but I'm gonna put this as best as I can. When I got took to jail and then prison, I fought everyone, even sometimes the COs. My rage wouldn't cut me no slack, no way, and I was a drunk, too, plus puttin' anything up my nose that would fit, which didn't help. There's more drugs in prison than on the street.

They put me in solitary twice, thirty days, sixty days, but when that didn't work, they just left me there, alone in a cell. About two years in was when the haunting began. There was me as a kid and what my father did to me. And there was you and what I did to you.

This come on me slow, like a feelin' that something's wrong, but over the years it wouldn't stop growin', just become bigger and bigger. Altogether, I spent fifteen years in solitary, and the two ghosts were my whole life by the end. What happened, what I did. I didn't want it to be, only I couldn't make it go away. After a time, I broke down. I'd get to cryin' and I couldn't stop. And there was no one gave a damn except the guy in the cell across the pod who called me a faggot.

I came around after a while, got stronger, the two ghosts now as much a part of me as my two eyes. But it still took another year before Admin decided that I was no longer violent and let me out of solitary. After that, I went straight into therapy. I didn't care what kind of therapy, substance, antiviolence, sex offender. I wanted an answer to a question I didn't know how to ask.

Carolyn, I am deeply sorry and deeply ashamed of what I done to you. I don't seek forgiveness, don't even ask it of the Lord, because what I done can't be forgiven. That I now believe. But I want you to know this. Nothing of what happened then was your fault. You were born under a bad sign named Hank Grand, and I hope with all my heart that you've escaped.

The session concludes as Halberstam returns the sheet of paper to his desk drawer. I get up to leave but can't resist a final jab. "Tell me, Doctor, which do you think is true? That my father's remorse is genuine? Or that the bastard's figured out what therapists want to hear?"

"Like you Martha, you and your sisters?" Halberstam shakes his head. "If I'm to help you," he finally says, his tone weary, "I must take you out of your comfort zone."

CHAPTER TWENTY
SERENA

Hank Grand's become the excuse, the gun held to my head by the prunes, no, you can't have the body, not even for a minute, not even if you remain indoors because he might come knocking and you're too weak to resist. I see my terrifying, necessary death everywhere. I see the big push-out, see the dug grave soon to be filled, see the graveside empty of mourners, goodbye and good riddance, whatever did we need that one for?

The prunes have murder in their hearts, always have, the purges relentless from earliest times, the knife in the back, the poison at the bottom of the glass. But in the end, they don't control the body, our decision maker hidden, always hidden, pronouncing life and death, existence and oblivion, its criteria unknown. So, here I am against the wishes of Victoria and Martha, who imagine themselves to have real power, out the door, into the street, skipping down the block. I'm wearing the harem pants I lucked upon in a Salvation Army thrift store and a T-shirt bearing the likeness of the photographer Margaret Bourke-White. Semi-reclined on a chaise lounge in a bathing suit, she holds a kitten against her chest, the contrast alluring, here gentle, but at work a warrior, the first woman combat photographer.

Bourke-White sought her own truth as I seek mine today on the streets of New York, the air saturated, scattered drops of rain as warm as blood falling across my face as I hustle up Flatbush Avenue to the Brooklyn Museum. I like to wander through the exhibitions at the museum, barely glancing at the individual pieces, the sculptures, the paintings, my goal only to draw breath after the endless hustle, like stepping into a Sixth Avenue church at rush hour, a familiar world closing behind you, a new world unfolding.

The museum charges $16 for admission, but the charge is merely suggested, a donation in support of a worthy cause. I shake my head as I walk past, then drift to the stairs and up, the only soul climbing, for all the rest it's elevator up, steps down. The galleries are crowded this afternoon, kids from summer camp looking like they'd rather be somewhere else, I don't see my father until I'm in a gallery created from the museum's storage area for expensive objects rich people can't find room for in their own homes. The exhibit is a maze of stacked glass cabinets, the panes reflecting reflections, images originating from everywhere and nowhere, yet I see him clearly, three or four levels deep but somehow looking at me, directly at me, measuring, measuring, who is it I find here, name the name of her soul.

I flee, my flight steady, a stroller's flight, looking here, looking there, but never stopped, thinking if I don't turn around I won't discover the torn fabric, the rent garment. The Egyptian room attracts me, naturally, this homage to the fear of death, of oblivion, not all the gold in the Nile valley enough to make life sweet, but then I happen upon the oddest of oddities, the carved image of a woman seated, one leg raised while a standing man feeds an enormous cock into her vagina. Egyptian pornograhy. Eleni would take these figures into her tomb if she were pharaoh, but I'm initially embarrassed and I instinctively look up at the painted ceiling, a soft blue circle filled with humans and animals and gods. I want to rise, to join these bodies, but I can't, my body now weighted with the heavy hand of my father as it drops to my shoulder.

"Hello, Carolyn. Hello, darlin'."

CHAPTER TWENTY-ONE

TINA

"Hello, Daddy. I knew you would come for me."

"That's right. It just had to happen, you and me. What are we without each other?" He leans in until I can smell his breath, the alcohol stench so familiar.

"How you've grown, little girl, grown to a woman. Me, I'm an old man with nothin' to do and nowhere to go. Except to you."

I send up a hopeless prayer, but I have no faith. Daddy looms above me and there's nothing I can do, not now, not before. His hand reaches out to gently stroke the side of my face, once, then again. I'm supposed to run, but I can't move. I'm frozen forever.

"You're not supposed to touch me."

"I know, honey, I know. We've had some hard times, the two of us, and they took you away from your daddy. But you were always a good girl."

Then why did you punish me, why, why, why, why, why, why . . . I have to ask. I can't ask. I say, "Yes, Daddy, I was always good." My insides tighten and twist and I feel the burning pain in my belly. I hear my father asking why I make him do this to his little girl. And me with never an answer.

Daddy steps back. People are looking at us. He takes my arm and leads me past a mummy's coffin, along a corridor to an open court, gigantic, with a glass floor and a window instead of a ceiling. I stop when he tugs on my arm and look up to find nothing changed. The body I occupy is still a little girl's body. Daddy has never been taller or stronger. My will is sucked up inside him. He gives. I receive. For all of my life, I never knew otherwise. I find myself wishing I'd grown up, knowing I have to grow up, that my girlhood is over, that it's finally time.

"I want you to come to me, little girl. Will you do that?"

I wonder how he knows it's me. I wonder if he waited and waited, never coming close until he was sure. I wonder what he'd say if it were Eleni or Martha. What would he say if he ran into Kirk? Now he speaks to me, only me.

"I will, Daddy. I'll come to you."

"Let me give you this, to help you remember." He takes a folded piece of yellow paper from his shirt pocket and tucks it into the small purse I carry. "Tonight, baby girl. Be on time, okay?"

"Yes, Daddy."

"Good, good." He smiles and nods as his fingers tighten on my arm. Harder and harder, until the tears well up. "Because you don't wanna make Daddy have to find you, Carolyn. You really don't."

CHAPTER TWENTY-TWO

KIRK

The first thing I do when I wake up is exchange the bikini panties and short nightgown for a pair of boxers emblazoned with prancing horses, well-worn jeans, and a Harvard University sweatshirt, sleeveless. I feel good, too good, and I wonder what went on last night, what adventure left the body fully charged. I get the coffee going, then head for the shower. A waste of time as it turns out. The body's been cleaned, scrubbed, and deodorized. The towel on the rack is damp, the washcloth draped over the faucet in the tub is still wet.

Was Eleni off on one of her adventures last night? The thought inspires a series of anatomically incorrect images and I'm already thinking about where I want to go this morning. I walk to the windows, looking for Hank Grand. I'm hoping to encounter our dad somewhere along the line. If I do, I'll find an excuse to cut the prick. That'll force the cops to take action whether they like it or not.

But there's no sign of him and I carry a mug of coffee to our one comfortable chair, turn on the TV, and jump from NY1 to ESPN. I'm a Yankee fan, and I want to catch up.

I'm just settling in when a knock at the front door brings me to full attention. I glance at the clock: 9:45.

"Who is it?"

"Police. Open the door, please."

I bring my eye to the peephole and find two men standing back about four feet. The short one looks annoyed, the taller one indifferent. Neither looks like Hank Grand.

"Show me some ID?"

That draws a scowl as the short one reaches into a back pocket. He's wearing a limp white shirt embellished with oval patches of sweat that extend from his armpits to the top of his swelling gut.

"Detective Greco." He flips a billfold open to reveal the gold badge carried by New York detectives. "Open the door, please."

I don't have a choice here and I know it. But I also want to know why they're here. More contact with the police? After Eleni's escapade? Yeah, that'll work.

I slide the chain off the hook, flip the lock and open the door. The second cop steps toward me. He's holding up his own badge, his expression soft, almost regretful.

"Detective Ortega, may we come in? It's about your father."

He glides past me without waiting for an answer, his fat partner following. Inside, they position themselves about five feet apart.

"You're Carolyn Grand, right?" the short one asks.

"Right."

He takes out a little notebook. "You've reported seeing your father since he was paroled. Twice, I think." He pauses to look up at me, like I'm supposed to answer some question he didn't ask. As he waits, his partner's dark eyes crisscross our apartment.

"And you're doing what?" I finally ask. "Following up?"

"In a manner of speaking, yes. Can you tell me when was the last time you saw your father?"

In fact, I don't know, not for sure. I've been absent for the last three days and have no idea what went on. Still, I have to guess, that or explain the whole multi business and admit that Carolyn Grand is psychotic. "A couple of days ago."

"Can you tell me under what circumstances?"

The tall cop slides away, toward our little table, the one covered with the memos we've been writing each other. I'm instantly pissed off, instantly wary. Whatever the fuckers want, it's far from routine.

"Hey, Detective Ortega, where are you going? I didn't—"

Greco touches my arm and I instinctively turn back to him. "We're here about your father, Ms. Grand. I'm sorry for your loss, but I have to tell you that your father is dead."

"What are you talkin' about?"

"I'm telling you that your father is deceased."

From the corner of my eye, I watch the second cop, Ortega, standing over the table, reading the memos without picking them up. I should complain, but I can't tear myself away from Detective Greco.

"How?" I ask. "How did he die?"

"I'm sorry to tell you this, but he was murdered."

Now it falls into place, their attitude, Ortega's wandering, the bullshit. In order to find us, they must have spoken to Hank Grand's parole officer. He would have reported the encounters and the nature of the crime that put Hank Grand in prison for twenty-seven years.

"You have to leave," I said.

"Don't you want us to find out who killed your father?"

"Actually, I don't give a flying fuck. But even if I did, I know nothing about my father's day-to-day life. I don't know who he saw or what he did. What I do know, on the other hand, is that your partner is searching my apartment without a fucking warrant. So . . ."

Clear as a bell, I hear Martha's voice in my ear. Call the lawyer, she tells me. The number's on the fridge.

As it turns out, I don't have to. I tell Ortega that I'm about to phone my lawyer, and he returns to his partner's side. Ortega's wearing a jacket but still looks cooler than Greco, who wipes his forehead with a damp handkerchief.

"Take my card, Ms. Grand," Ortega says. "If you can think of anything that might help, I'd appreciate a call. My cell number's on the back." He hands me his card and smiles. "Oh, before we go, one more thing. Please tell us where you were between nine o'clock last night and two this morning? For the record."

I haven't any idea, not even a memory of a memory. But again, I know I have to answer. "Home, detective. Home alone."

I let the two cops out, then almost collapse as the implications sink in. Another encounter with the cops, the cops obviously including us in their list of suspects, our lives already under the scrutiny of the courts. I walk over to our miniscule dining table and start to examine the memos. Most of them I've seen, all except for an unfolded sheet of yellow paper, maybe six inches square. Across the middle, in block letters: 344 HUNTINGTON STREET.RM. 307.

Shit.

CHAPTER TWENTY-THREE

MARTHA

We're celebrating, the whole family except for Tina, at Coney Island. I'm nominally in charge, but the body's more or less wandering. The voices running through its brain might belong to any family on a summer outing and the weather's perfect. The temperature's in the low eighties, the sun in and out of glowing clouds, and there's a lush breeze coming off the water. As if, Serena whispers, the universe celebrates with us.

We listen to the chatter of other sightseers as they pass by. The swelling clatter of the roller coasters. The screams of the passengers. The distant pounding of the surf. Yeah, we've been outcasts for all of our life. Only now, for this brief time, we feel as though we actually belong. Just another city dweller—crazy, true, but ya can't tell—enjoying a summer day at the beach.

Eleni teases me as we go. Indicating this or that young woman, suggesting I move on her.

"Take it from the voice of experience, you approach enough girls, one of them will say yes."

"And that would be you, Eleni," Kirk jumps in. "The one they finally got to after everyone else said no."

Eleni laughs. "Better late than never."

Serena has been mostly quiet, but I can feel her breath in my ear. Nobody wants to hear a new-age rant, but I'm glad she's here. Hank Grand's haunted us for thirty-seven years and now his spirit's burning in hell. We know that his plea, the one Halberstam read to Martha, was pure bullshit. Did he hope to lure us in when he wrote it? Or was it meant only for his parole officer? The only thing I'm sure about is that contrition is an emotion Hank Grand never felt. Maybe he faked it well enough to fool his parole officer, but a sadist is a sadist and our daddy was addicted to pain. Not his own, of course.

So, if anyone on this planet has a right to be happy, it's definitely my psycho family: Victoria, Serena, Eleni, Kirk and Tina. We've fought battle after battle in what amounts to a war for survival. The years of therapy definitely provided insight. But they did not provide the tools we needed to fix the broken parts. We had to find those tools on our own. We're still looking.

Bottom line, our joys will always be as temporary as our individual lives. Better take them while we can because there's a dark side to Hank Grand's termination. A truck on a one-lane road coming right for us. Dodge right? Dodge left? Make a mistake and we're roadkill.

Kirk loves crime shows and crime fiction, which he reads online. Homicide cops, he was eager to explain, focus on three items when they investigate a murder: means, motive, and opportunity. We have a pair of undeniable motives: revenge and self-preservation. We had opportunity as well, which the cops already know if Ortega read the address on the table. As for the means, if any of us knows how our father was killed, she or he isn't ready to admit it. Each of us claims innocence. That proves exactly nothing, of course, not even to Serena. But I will say this in our defense. Kirk went through the apartment after the cops left, searching for bloodstains. He examined every item of clothing, dirty or clean, but found nothing.

Unfortunately, we can't bring ourselves to believe that innocence will protect us. We can't because we know the court will never end our medical supervision as long as the cops suspect us. And if we're arrested? If we're charged, even if we're acquitted, we can look forward to long-term confinement in a mental hospital. The medical board deciding our fate doesn't require proof beyond a reasonable doubt. There's no jury, either, to make the final decision. Only a panel of doctors and career bureaucrats assigned to judge whether or not we present a danger to ourselves or society or their immediate interests. An arrest would pretty much conclude the debate. So, we believe, all of us.

It's the end of the month and we're almost broke. I've got $20 in the pocket of my respectable shorts and a MetroCard with three rides on it. Enough to get home and to keep our next appointment with Halberstam. Kirk and Eleni have their hearts set on one of the roller coasters, the Cyclone or the

Thunderbolt. Unfortunately, both are in Luna Park where the most basic admission is $22. So, that's not happening and we settle for a ride on the Wonder Wheel, a Ferris wheel with cars on tracks that slide across the face of the wheel.

The view from the top across the Brooklyn flatlands is stupendous, the sudden shifts sufficiently alarming to coax a squeal from Eleni. But it's over soon enough. We head for Nathan's and its famous hotdogs, detouring to the water's edge for a barefoot walk in the foam. As we go along, I sense our brief escape fading away. Maybe Dr. Halberstam's receptionist sealed the deal when she called this morning to announce that our appointment has been moved up. The doctor will see us at nine tomorrow morning. Maybe our celebration marks little more than a desperate attempt to make something from nothing.

We're a lot more sober as we eat our hotdogs, as we drink our soda. We're standing at the edge of the boardwalk, looking out over the sand at the ocean beyond. But it's not the ocean, Victoria corrects. We're looking at the waters of the lower bay. The Atlantic Ocean begins on the other side of the Rockaways.

Without warning, we begin to squabble. As much as Serena's spiritual diatribes repel me, Victoria's college-acquired knowledge repels Kirk and Eleni. And they're not shy about letting her know it. Voices swirl about each other for a moment, unintelligible, chaotic. I bring my hand to my ears, the gesture as futile as it is stupid. Eleni's now demanding possession of our body. She claims she'll treat it to a final celebration a lot more celebratory than riding a Ferris wheel.

I object. Victoria objects. Don't we have enough problems already? Kirk demands his own turn, claiming he's been denied his fair share for so long he sometimes forgets that he exists. Our voices rise in intensity and the adrenalin begins to flow. I have no authority here, my voice one of many, my control an illusion. I know it, they know it. Then, in an instant, I'm gone.

CHAPTER TWENTY-FOUR

SERENA

I flow through New York's underground bloodstream, the arteries, veins, and capillaries that transport the city's basic energy: steam and water and sewage, TV signals through cable and fiber optic lines, electricity, telephone, and enough natural gas to cook millions of family dinners. Water pours first through twenty-foot tunnels, is stepped down from main to main, finally emerges drop by drop from a showerhead to run into drains, to collect in pipes, rushing faster and faster, to sewage treatment plants or into the rivers. I flow now through an artery that transports human energy, a crowded subway train, human on human, male and female, old and young, black, white, and brown, predator and prey, eyes averted, always in a hurry, carry me forward.

Humans flow, flow both ways, in and out at every stop, I've got a seat and can afford to watch, to practice the art of seeing without looking, privacy in public. At the other end of the car a tall heavy man hangs on to the pole with both hands as he makes his passionate pleading case, as he begs to finally be understood. Alone, shunned, no fellow passenger within ten feet, his appeals fall on deaf ears. And yet he, too, flows.

A woman boards at Prospect Avenue pushing a double stroller, both seats occupied by toddlers barely out of infancy, a third child trailing behind clutches her belt. Very short, less than five feet tall with a long oval face and aquiline nose, the woman forces her way onto the crowded car, other passengers resenting the intrusion, the stroller, the demand for space. The woman's mouth is set, though her dark eyes are cast downward. This is something she must do, move her family through this artery at this time, she absorbs the ire, even a half-whispered comment designed to be overheard: "Children having children. Why do they come here?"

I see her and I see us, every day a struggle far from any homeland, much too young to be so weary. I want to reach out, to offer my hope, a gift, finally, in a land where nothing is freely given. I don't, I can't, I won't. I ride to my stop, get off, climb the stairs, take a second to absorb the angled sunlight, and walk away.

There's a man standing at the bottom of the steps in front of my building—a cop, it's obvious—probably the young one described in Kirk's memo. Kirk left out the part about the wide shoulders and narrow hips, the hawk's nose, the tan skin, the narrow dark eyes that reach into me, searching, searching, searching until finally they reveal a flicker of doubt. Who am I? Not the Carolyn Grand he met yesterday morning, but who is he dealing with, what crazed entity does he intend to question? I feel sorry for him, so bewildered in a profession where confidence is the key to success.

I stop when he glides into my path. "And you are?" I demand.

A smile starts, then just as quickly stops and I know he's aware, however dimly, of our diagnosis. No details, of course, what with patients entitled to confidentiality, but a rough diagnosis, the same diagnosis that's followed us for the past fifteen years, multiple personality, batshit crazy.

"Detective second-grade Bobby Ortega." The smile finally makes it all the way to his face. Whatever he's thinking, it amuses him. He offers his hand and I take it, imagining the emotions and sensations sure to flow through Eleni's mind and body when she finally meets him, his smile so much younger than I expect.

"And you are?" he says.

Ortega's testing the waters, but I'm not a fish and I don't swim into view. I answer without hesitation. "Carolyn Grand."

"I knocked on your door, but there was no one home."

I hear Victoria, her tone sharp: Don't tell him anything. Don't be an idiot.

"I spent the afternoon at Coney Island with the ocean, the cool breeze, the rides, and the people, a bubbling stew that only became more and more flavorful as the time passed."

His smile jumps to a full laugh, but his eyes remain cold and calculating. "You're trying too hard," he says.

"Or not hard enough." I shift my weight, prepared to walk around him. "What do you want of me? How can I be of service?"

"Well, when I notified you of your father's murder . . ."

The sharp edge he puts to the word "murder" places me on notice. I think he means to frighten me, but in this case I have the perfect alibi.

"You told me," he continues, "that you were home that evening and all night. Can you tell me exactly when you arrived home?"

"I can't."

His eyebrows rise. "You can't?" he repeats.

"No, I'm sorry, but I can't."

"And why is that?"

"Because I didn't exist."

Again he smiles, again the hopeful smile of a very young child, mischievous, genuinely amused. He steps out of my way, then continues speaking as I climb the stoop. "Funny thing, Ms. Grand, but I've made a hundred notifications over the years and the first thing family members want to know is how it happened. The only people who don't ask, in my experience, are people who already know."

There's nothing to be gained from this encounter. I pass by, up the steps, through the door, and into the hallway. Doyle stands next to Marshal by the elevator. They look at me and laugh.

"You meet the cop?" Doyle's arms are folded above his sagging belly.

"Yes."

"Know what he wanted?" He points to the security camera over the elevator doors. "He wanted the data, night before yesterday, from six at night until six in the morning. Pushy, too, the asshole."

I'm not good at lying and I didn't lie to Detective Ortega, which means exactly nothing because if one of us killed our father, all will be punished.

"Did you give it to him?"

"Nothin' to give, Serena," Marshal says, the sound of my name on his lips comforting. "The system hasn't worked in five years. I offered to repair it when I first moved in, but Nazari told me that he wasn't putting out one dime to fix a system that he knew didn't work when he bought the building."

CHAPTER TWENTY-FIVE

ELENI

I'm not big on asking why and I don't ask this time. It's eight o'clock in the morning and I'm off to keep our day-after-Daddy's-murder appointment with the dear doctor. Lucky him, lucky me. I've been looking forward to the challenge for a long time.

There's nobody around for once, nobody to pepper me with advice. There's only Doyle. He's preparing the garbage for pickup, moving small bags of trash into larger bags. The job is unpleasant enough, even when it's cool. At the end of August, after a few days in the sun, the stink is almost visible.

As I pass, Doyle stops what he's doing and stares at me, a wet bag of garbage in one hand. But he doesn't say anything until I'm ten feet away. Then he empties the contents of his heart.

"At least I'm not crazy."

I shake my ass at him and keep on going.

Most men, like Doyle, are afraid of me. Most women hate me. I'm too much of a challenge for the man who does your taxes and yet I'm the focus of his erotic fantasies. Me and women like me. That's fine by Eleni Grand. I have little interest in women—my sisters are hassle enough—and I want to eliminate the incompetent. Maybe that's what happens when you only get laid every three weeks, all that pent-up demand.

I'm guessing the man who steps out of the dear doctor's office building isn't afraid of me—or anyone. He's wearing a suit and tie, the suit tan, the tie only a shade darker. His stride, as he turns toward me, is perfectly balanced. Not catlike, not artificial, but naturally light. His expression projects the same attitude. Entirely in control, yet entirely relaxed. No worries in the world. And if the planes of his brow and jaw are a bit too strong, I'm encouraged by a line of pits in the hollow beneath his cheekbones, the remnants of a long-vanquished acne. His self-confidence has been earned, not given.

Right away, I'm thinking to hell with the dear doctor. It's been . . . I have to think for a moment before I can put a time to when I last felt the touch of a man. More than two weeks since I lay next to a lover, physically spent, only to have him roll onto one arm and gently kiss me on the mouth. Too long, too long.

The tender caress of a man is something the prunes have never known. Not from the day they were born. Never.

"Ms. Grand?"

My brain doesn't want to let go of the fantasy and I freeze for a few seconds before I recall the memo left by Serena. The man is a cop, the one who confronted Serena last night. She described him as "intimidating," but I've been with enough cops to know the front they project comes of long practice. If you know which buttons to push, you can get behind it.

"And you are?" I ask.

The question provokes a smile. "I think I heard this song before. Last night, in fact."

"You'll probably hear it again before you're through. My apologies, but we're crazy, which I suppose you already know, being as you've spoken to our therapist."

He doesn't rise to the bait. Instead, still smiling, he extends a hand, palm up. "Detective Ortega, at your service."

He clasps my hand, his touch as gentle as it is erotic. The prick intends it, too. I can see it in his eyes, in his soft smile, a challenge to equal my own. I'm not playing anymore. There's no point.

I finally remember the name Serena included in her memo. Bobby Ortega. I lift my head and his eyes lock on to mine. He's not trying to dominate me, just taking a hard look. I leave my palm in his hand for a second too long, then glance at my watch. His eyes dip, then rise, nose to toes and back again. I'm wearing a sheer white blouse and my blue skirt is just tight enough to provide my butt with the small lift it needs. I'm thirty-seven, with enough bulges and sags to prove it. Attractive is the aim these days, not teenage street hooker.

Ortega's smile expands and he says, "I'm glad I ran into you, Ms. Grand. I was going to stop by your apartment anyway. Now I can save myself the trip. Your father's body hasn't been formally identified and I'm hoping you'll come to the morgue this afternoon, around three."

I don't give a shit about my father's body. What I'm wondering is whether the cop does either. His tone is steady enough, but the smile tells another story. I read that smile as a question I could answer now, but where's the fun in that?

"It's too hot to take the subway. You'd have to pick me up, drive me there and back."

"I will, definitely. And I appreciate the favor."

I've been with quite a few cops. They make good lovers, the ones I've picked out at least. They're aggressive, but never cross the line between forceful and forced. Now I'm looking at Ortega the way he's looking at me. I'm measuring the swell of his chest, the flat belly, the smooth line from his lower ribs to his hips. All that concealed power.

Victoria's voice sounds in my ear at that moment, as if she'd been there all along. "Are you crazy? We're suspects in a murder he happens to be investigating?"

I make the same answer I've been making for years. No risk, no reward.

"Around three? Consider it done?"

He smiles and steps aside. "I assume you have an appointment with Dr. Halberstam."

"Sad, but true." I walk past him, then turn into the entrance to Halberstam's building. I'm not expecting anything beyond a careful scrutiny of my ass, but Ortega ups the stakes.

"Were you at the Golden Inn Hotel last night?" he asks.

I understand the question to be part of the challenge—in his eyes, in mine. Foreplay with a razor's edge. "Is that where he was killed?"

"Yeah."

"Well, I couldn't have been there."

"Why is that?"

"Because I didn't exist."

"That's another one I heard yesterday."

I open the door and step inside before he can ask a follow-up question, one I'd prefer not to answer: Have you *ever* been to the Golden Inn Hotel?

CHAPTER TWENTY-SIX

ELENI

Only Serena got it right. Victoria, Martha, even Kirk, they all missed. Dear doctor's stare isn't predatory or piercing. He's trying much too hard for that. No, his stare is supremely artificial and I know, like Serena instinctively knew, that he passed his adolescence dreaming of girls he never had the courage to approach. Halberstam's the ultimate nerd, the one who stood by the fence at the back of the schoolyard. Now he's got real power. Now he's dangerous. Now he's out to get even.

I'd be afraid, but I don't do fear.

I'm in the chair described by my brother and sisters. The submissive chair. Fine with me. I allowed my dress to slide up a bit when I sat down, so now, with my legs crossed, I know he can track the underside of my thighs almost to the swell of my ass. I've pulled my shoulders back as well. We don't have the biggest boobs in town, but an asset's an asset.

I watch the disappointment build as he continues to stare at me. I've offered a dare he hasn't the courage to accept and we both know it. We both know that I've measured him out, that I've found him wanting just like every other woman in his life. Kirk was an idiot to suggest we keep the dear doctor in line with sex. No, the dear doctor's a walking billboard for erectile dysfunction related to performance anxiety. I need to lead him to a line he can't cross. Lead him to the line, but keep him on the safe side. That way he can go home with his fantasies intact.

I find myself considering Bobby Ortega, wondering if there's a challenge he won't accept. Wondering if there's a challenge he's prepared to offer that I'd refuse. Finally, a thought wiggles its way into my horny brain. Ortega knows who we are, knows the woman he met last night, Serena, is not the woman he met this morning. He knows and he doesn't care. This is new for me and I feel exposed as never before, exposed and vulnerable. I recall asking a man I met at a street fair if he'd like some crazy sex. I might have asked Ortega the same question in the same words, the meanings entirely different. He's promised to pick me up at three—a trip to the morgue—but if I have my way, the two of us will never leave the apartment.

"Am I finally speaking to Eleni?"

"That's me."

"I should tell you, right away, that I was just visited by a policeman, a detective who claimed to be investigating the murder of your father. Yet here you sit, as if your father's death means nothing at all. Nothing positive, nothing negative. You're not happy, you're not sad."

"Family relations . . . not my focus. As for his murder, well sometimes bad things do happen to bad people."

"Really? Well, we can talk about that later on. Your reaction." He turns to a notebook on his desk, thumbs through the pages, lays it flat. "This is our first meeting, Eleni, and it's been long in coming. Too long, considering that you're the one who precipitated the events that brought Carolyn Grand to my office. Victoria, for instance, at our first meeting, told me that you were 'promiscuous.'" He stops to review his notes for a moment. "And Martha didn't deny that you were promiscuous. No, she defended your right to be promiscuous, as so many New York women are. Now I want to hear it from you and please keep your account accurate. Let me add that the police investigating your father's murder have also contacted the court and the physicians on the board are very nervous. So . . ."

He lays his elbows on the desk and leans forward, his genial expression in sharp contrast to the threat he delivered. But Martha was right to defend me. I did nothing to be ashamed of.

"Except for a few isolated hours," I begin, my tone sultry, "I'd been out of the body for more than a week before I took full possession. You can feel that. You can know you'll be around for a while. So, I was especially horny and I had the time and"—I lean forward, just a bit—"I left our apartment fully expecting to get laid. That's about as raw as I can make it. My first preference was for one of the after-work bars near Wall Street. That wasn't happening, because it was the end of the month and we were broke, as usual. So, I decided to walk around a bit, take my chances, hope for the best.

Maybe twenty minutes later, I see the cop, or the guy who turned out to be a cop, leaning against the wall of a bodega on President Street."

I'm about to describe his appearance—about thirty-five, suitably trim and rugged—when I realize that I'd describe Ortega exactly the same way. Now I can only wish he was there instead of the asshole I stumbled on to.

"I walked up and propositioned him, simple as that."

"What did you say, exactly?"

The demand comes as no surprise and I give Halberstam his cheap thrill. I'm careful to add just enough sneer to expose my disdain, along with enough leg to keep his attention where it needs to be.

"I didn't have a lot of time, so I kept it simple. I stood right in front of him, looked into his eyes for a moment and said, 'If you follow me into that alley, I guarantee you'll come out with a pair of empty balls.'"

The dear doctor rocks back a few inches and I'm sure I touched one of those closely held fantasies he'll never make real. Fuck him.

"Short and sweet, Doctor. He hauled out his badge, which he wore on a chain beneath his shirt, and demanded ID. I produced our New York resident card, but it wasn't enough and he decided, all on his own, to run my name through a database that included individuals committed in the past to a New York psychiatric hospital. Carolyn Grand popped up and now what was he gonna do? Am I really crazy? Can he take a chance?" I grinned, displaying my hands, palms up. "When in doubt, refer any problem to a higher authority, in this case Sergeant Brady, his immediate supervisor. Brady questioned me for about ten minutes and I could see in his eyes that I propositioned the wrong cop. If I'd been lucky enough to run into Brady first, we'd be in the alley now, rutting behind a dumpster like stray dogs. That couldn't happen. Too many witnesses. So, Brady eventually picked the one sure way to handle me without it coming back to bite him. He shipped me off to a locked ward at Kings County Hospital. Let the shrinks figure it out."

The dear doctor's eyes jump around, from feature to feature, across my face, finally to the hemline of my skirt. I lean back in the chair, giving him enough space to enjoy his daydreams. The gleam in his eye tells me that he liked my story, which contained several deliberate lies. What I actually said to the cop, for example, was equally blatant, but much less offensive. I even added a touch of humor.

"I've got two hours to kill, baby. So, if you've got a place we can be alone, you can have me any way you want, fried, poached, hard-boiled, soft-boiled or sunny-side up."

In the end, it hardly mattered because the cop reacted in the same way. And so did Sergeant Brady when he finally arrived. But there was no gleam in Brady's eyes when he approached me, and no thought of rutting behind a dumpster. What's more, I was gone before Brady called in the paramedics, replaced by poor Victoria.

The dear doctor bangs away at his computer's keyboard for a moment before looking up. "Do you appreciate the risk you took? Propositioning a perfect stranger?"

"I took very little risk." For once I tell the truth. "Take this from a woman who's been there. You don't choose the man who wants to slap you around. He chooses you. And he doesn't throw a rope around you and drag you off. He charms you first, then flips the switch when he gets you alone."

Dear doctor's ready for me this time. "Even if I concede that you're less likely to get into trouble if you choose randomly, that doesn't eliminate the possibility that you'll choose the wrong man. And not someone who merely 'slaps you around' but someone who'll kill you."

I give it a beat before responding. "I once read an article about women who fly rescue helicopters into combat zones. Bullets flying everywhere, rocket-propelled grenades fired from rooftops. 'This is for me.' That's what I thought. Or it would be if I had a remote shot at a normal life. Which, of course . . ."

Dear doctor gets to his feet, looks at his notes for a moment. Then he comes around his desk to perch on the edge closest to me. I see genuine curiosity in his eyes and I know I'm ahead of the game. I've challenged him, drawn him to the line, but I haven't pulled him across. Even if I know, I won't tell.

"In theory," he says, "there's no time limit for therapy. Therapist and patient continue on as long as the sessions are productive. Your case, on the other hand, demands an immediate judgment. The detective who interviewed me, though he refused to answer directly when I asked if you were a suspect, said that he was 'looking at anyone who had contact with Hank Grand since he was released.' That certainly includes you."

"That's true, but I only saw my father for a few seconds in a supermarket. There was no actual contact." I recross my legs, chin up, looking directly into his eyes. "But if you're asking me if I killed my father, the answer is no. I couldn't have because, you see, I didn't exist."

"Ah, the default response. I didn't exist. Do you know how many times I've heard that?"

"I wouldn't know because—"

"Because you didn't exist. I believe you, too, Eleni, but I'm not sure the review board will. In any event, painful though it is, I have to be frank here. Your continued freedom hangs by a thread. The judge and the doctors on the review board, even the administrators at Kings County, they're preparing the statements they'll release to the press if you're arrested. Statements explaining why they discharged you in the first place." He glances at his watch. "I want you to know that I'm defending you as best I can, but my opinion is far from binding. If I were in your shoes, I'd find a good lawyer and keep a very low profile. Don't give the board an excuse to pull the plug."

I stand up. Time to go. The dear doctor's startled at first, but then folds his arms across his chest.

"You seem to think we should be grateful," I tell him. "Thank you for releasing us from this prison you call a hospital. Not me, not my sisters, not my brother. We know we never should have been committed in the first place."

"That," he declares with a quick shake of his head, "is not what I hoped to hear. You're telling me that you intend to take the same risks in the future that you did in the past. Would you please explain, before you go, exactly what you hope to achieve?"

"Orgasms, Doctor. As in more than one."

I head for the door, thinking I'd gotten the last laugh, but the dear doctor's a step ahead this time. He raises a finger, bringing me to a halt.

"One more thing before you leave, Eleni. You told me that you couldn't have killed your father because you didn't exist on the night your father was killed. But if you didn't exist, you can't know what happened. You can't know who inhabited Carolyn Grand's body, nor where they went, nor what they did. Not unless someone confessed. Did that happen, Eleni? Did someone confess?"

"Not to me."

"Would you tell me if they did?"

That brings forth my best and brightest smile. "Please, Dr. Halberstam, do you really think I'm that crazy?"

CHAPTER TWENTY-SEVEN
MARTHA

Victoria's been after me to call our lawyer and I finally dial the number right after I finish lunch. Two off-brand hotdogs courtesy of a food pantry. I don't expect to reach Malaya Castro on the first try, but for once I get lucky.

I've been half expecting your call," she says once I identify myself.

"You heard?"

"Late yesterday afternoon, I received a call from, let's see. . . ." After a moment of silence, she comes back on. Her tone, as usual, is a bit too cheery. "A call from Dr. Plink at the medical review board. He told me your father had been murdered and the board was concerned with your status."

"What'd you tell him?"

"I told him that until you were arrested and charged, Legal Aid would fight recommitment."

"Does that mean you think we'll be charged? That you've spoken to the cops?"

Malaya laughs out loud. "Carolyn, the last thing any cop wants to do is talk to a suspect's lawyer. And besides, I only represent you on the medical issue."

"C'mon, Malaya, are we suspects or not?"

"Have they read your rights to you?"

I'm suddenly weary. Weary and afraid. I feel like the last domino in a long line. I can hear the clatter of falling dominoes, but I can't move. I can't get out of the way.

"No, they haven't."

"Okay, bad habit, I sometimes speak off the top of my head. You're not formally a suspect until your rights are read to you. And maybe the cops have someone else they're looking at. Maybe you're barely on their radar."

I draw a breath. Moment of truth, ally or not. Let's find out where we stand. "If necessary, can we say that you represent us?"

"You can ask for a lawyer at any time," Malaya responds. "You never have to talk to the cops. As for me representing you, if the cops should read your rights to you, stop them when they get to the part about you having a right to an attorney. Tell them you want to exercise that right. That should bring the questioning to a stop without you having to call anyone. On the other hand, if you decide to talk to them, and I sincerely hope you won't, you should know that they'll probably lie to you. They'll claim to have evidence they don't have, eyewitnesses they don't have, video they don't have. And it's legal, Carolyn. They're allowed to lie to you until you don't know up from down."

I take a second to process the message. "And if we don't talk to them? If we tell them to go fuck themselves? What then?"

"In that case, if they have enough evidence to show probable cause, they'll arrest you. If not, they'll let you go." She hesitates for just a moment. "Look, if worse comes to worse and the cops don't let up after you ask for a lawyer, call me. I can't represent you at trial or arraignment, but the cops won't know that. If I tell them to stop questioning you, they'll stop."

CHAPTER TWENTY-EIGHT
MARTHA

I'm still trying to process that last bit when someone knocks on the door. I look through the little peephole. There's a man well away from the door, a cop. Not the fat cop, the other one.

"Who is it?"

"Detective Ortega." His expression doesn't change and his tone remains calm. Like he knows exactly who he's dealing with.

"What do you want?"

"Ms. Grand, would you please open the door. I'm not going to bite you. I promise."

I open the door and he moves a little closer. He doesn't have to shout now. "We met this morning as you arrived for your appointment with Dr. Halberstam. You agreed to identify your father's body. You even insisted that I drive you to the morgue and back." He glances at his watch. "Three o'clock, right on time."

Eleni strikes again. How she could have made the appointment in the first place is beyond . . . No, that's not right. Eleni wants to screw the cop and she hoped to be the one who answered the door. If so, they would have been a long time getting to the morgue. But Eleni's not here and she didn't leave a note and what the hell am I going to do now?

"What if say no?"

I expect him to argue that I've already committed myself. I expect a display of righteous indignation, but he simply shrugs. Only his eyes give him away and I imagine him hunched over his notebook later on, committing his evaluation to paper.

"If you say no, it's no. We'll have to find someone else."

He waits, I wait, we both wait. Until I feel an unexpected impulse move me. I suddenly want to see Hank Grand's body. I want to see him cold, the blood drained from his face. I want to look into his dead blank eyes and know he can never hurt us again.

"Yeah, alright," I finally say. "I'll go with you."

Ortega opens the back door of his unmarked Ford and I slide onto the seat. I'm wearing loose jeans, a pullover jersey large enough to conceal my breasts and a pair of beat-up sneakers. Ortega has to know that I'm not the Carolyn Grand he met this morning, but he's not giving his disappointment away. That alone rings a hundred warning bells.

I decide to keep my mouth shut. I won't be the first to speak. Neither, apparently, will Ortega. Except for a few muttered curses—at a bus that could pull to the curb but stops in mid lane—he maintains a stony silence. Our route takes us over the Brooklyn Bridge, then north on Centre Street through the East Village into Midtown. There are lights on every block along with the usual obstacles. Double-parked trucks, Con Ed digs, new construction. I'm reacting like I'm in a cab watching the meter tick, growing more and more impatient with each delay.

I give up as we pass Houston Street, speaking for the first time. I've shifted in my seat so that I can watch him in the rearview mirror. I'm expecting something, maybe a triumphant smirk. But outside of raising his chin at the sound of my voice, Ortega's expression doesn't change.

"You spoke to Dr. Halberstam?" I intend to make a statement, but it emerges as a question. I remind myself that I'm Martha and I have to stand up for my siblings.

"Yes, briefly."

"Did he tell you that we're crazy?"

"You keep saying we, instead of I. Is there more than one of you?"

"Halberstam didn't reveal our diagnosis?"

"Dr. Halberstam was a base we had to touch. But shrinks never give you much and neither did Halberstam."

I know, instinctively, that Ortega's playing me. He's forcing me to carry the conversation, dragging the words out of my mouth. But I continue anyway, even though I feel like I'm about to gush. Not my way, not at all.

"He must have told you something."

"Only that you spent a few days in the Kings County psych ward and you're now in therapy."

"What about his attitude?"

Ortega taps the steering wheel with a finger as he considers the question. "Ya know, the shrinks I've interviewed are mostly hard reads. They've got this look, very professional, how can I help you, goodbye. But Halberstam . . . I thought for a second that he seemed . . . I don't know, proprietary, maybe. Or possessive."

I let my weight drop to the seat back. Ortega nailed Halberstam, no question. Still, I can't shake the feeling that I'm being manipulated. I want Ortega to know who we are. I want him to know that meeting Serena one day, Eleni the next, and me today isn't about playing a game. It's not about deception.

And maybe I'm begging, too.

"Our official diagnosis is dissociative identity disorder. There's more than one of us."

"That's like multiple personalities."

"Like that movie, *The Three Faces of Eve*."

"I was thinking *Split*, actually. You know, where the multi kills his therapist."

In a moment, we're both laughing. Not for long and no deep guffaws. Not enough to even put me off my guard. Still, I'm starting to think I might actually like this guy. I watch him tap the steering wheel again, a tell for sure. He's measuring his words before he speaks.

"Do you have like different names?" he asks.

"Look, detective, I just thought you should know what you're dealing with. The rest of it is our business. But, yes, we have different names."

"And you are?"

"Martha."

"Okay, so tell me, Martha, where were you on the night your father was killed? Did you exist?"

I laugh again. I've been led to water and now I'll drink. Good move, one that puts Halberstam to shame.

"I did exist and I was home all night. You want it step by step? After dinner, I set up the ironing board in front of the TV and went to work. That was around seven. Then I watched *Modern Family* and *American Housewife* while I ironed blouses, skirts, and pants. Sitcoms fascinate me, by the way. They're so far removed from the lives we've lived, they seem like science fiction."

I pause for a moment while he guides the car into a parking space reserved for cops on official business. His eyes are dark and hard to read inside the car, but I don't sense hostility.

"At ten," I tell him, "I switched to the local news. You know, a police shooting in the Bronx, video of a robbery in Brooklyn, weather, weather, weather. I wasn't watching the clock, but I'd say I was in bed by ten thirty." I shake my head, still trying to read Ortega. "For certain, I never opened the front door."

"Well, if you did, we'll definitely know. The security cameras in this building don't work, but there's a camera across the street that covers the entrance to your building. We won't get our hands on it until this evening, maybe tomorrow morning." He smiles. "No offense, by the way. Like me visiting your therapist, it's just another base to cover. Plus, you knew where your father would be that night. You had the address of the Golden Inn Hotel lying on your little table. In plain view."

Despite the last part, I brighten at the thought. Redemption, or at least the possibility. If we're eliminated as suspects, there's no new reason to commit us. "So, if you watch the tape and don't find Carolyn Grand, that's it. We're clear?"

He shakes his head as he pops the locks and opens his door. "The fire escape in your kitchen leads to an alley separating your building from the one to the north. The alley runs all the way between your street, South Portland Avenue, and South Oxford Street to the east. There's no security camera back there, just low gates at either end. They wouldn't present much of a challenge to someone really determined."

He doesn't add "really motivated" because he doesn't have to.

CHAPTER TWENTY-NINE

TINA

Daddy's skin is gray. His lips are the color of gristle and his eyes have shrunk down into his head like something was pulling at them. I know what that something is. It's death.

If death goes on long enough, death claims everything in the body, even the bones, the fingernails, the hair. That's what they taught me in school.

Daddy made me go to school. He told me I had to because if I didn't go to school the city would come around asking why. Then they would take me away and sell me and I'd be a slave forever, even when I grew up.

So, I decided to go to school and Daddy got me all dressed on my first day. He took my hand, but he didn't open the door. He knelt down and said, "Listen close, Carolyn. You're gonna go to school, but you can't tell nobody about the special things we do together. Nobody."

"Okay, I won't."

He shook his head and grabbed my chin and forced me to look into his eyes. I was afraid of his eyes, but I had to look anyway.

He said, "Do you remember Pancho?"

Pancho was the name of the dog we had once. He was always nice to me, but one day he tried to bite Daddy. So Daddy tied him to a pipe in the basement and killed him. Daddy made me watch. He said, "This is what happens when you're bad. This is what you get."

He hit Pancho with a golf club. Hit him again and again and again. Pancho screamed for a long time. Then he whimpered for a long time. Then he died. I remember watching his chest rise and fall, faster and faster. I remember that his tongue was hanging all the way out and it was covered with blood. I remember that when he died, his eyes looked like Daddy's do now.

"What happened to Pancho could happen to you, little girl. Yes, it could. Anything can happen to bad little girls and there's nothing they can do about it."

I didn't tell anyone. My first year and my second year in school. I didn't talk to anyone except teachers when they asked a question and I always sat by myself and I never looked at anyone. I wanted to be the invisible girl, but they found me anyway. First a few. Freak, freak, freak. Then everyone. Freak, freak, freak. Pinches, shoves, yanks came next, but they weren't anything at all compared to Daddy. Alone, though, always alone. At home, at school. Always. They could smell it on me.

I told in third grade. I told Mrs. Vallardi. She was my counselor and she said it would be all better if I talked about my problems at home. She knew something was wrong she said. I couldn't fool her. So, I told.

I told and I told and they took Daddy away and they gave me to the Acevedas in the Bronx. The Acevedas were nicer than Daddy. If I did my work, if I was a good, good girl, they never punished me.

CHAPTER THIRTY
MARTHA

I come awake slowly, aware of sounds, a mumbling and the sobs of a woman. My first instinct is to move away, to create distance. Yet I stay where I am, my body not yet under my control. Seconds pass, a minute, before I realize that the body wracked with sobs is my own and the mumbling is a clumsy attempt by Ortega to offer comfort. His arms are wrapped around my shoulders and my head is against his chest and my tears have soaked his blue shirt.

Horrified, I push him away, hard enough so that he stumbles back. I've never felt a man's arms around me, never known comfort from a man or a woman. I'm not about to start now. No fucking way.

"Martha?" Ortega's mouth is set in a line, his eyes narrowed. I don't know what to make of his expression. Don't know what Tina—and it could only be Tina, crying on a man's shoulder—might have told him. But I do know that I have to reply.

"Yes."

"And before?"

"Tina." I turn away to straighten my clothes. "She remembers." The truth is far more complicated, but I don't explain. "It's not like she has a choice."

I turn back toward Ortega, glimpsing as I turn a fixed image on a monitor. The monitor's positioned on a shelf behind the cop and it's displaying a single image: my father's head. He doesn't seem to me very changed. His skin is grayish and his eyes are somewhat shrunken and his lips are colorless. But all in all, he seems oddly undamaged. Not that I expect him to get up. I know he's dead, that death has claimed him. Removed from our future, he no longer frightens me.

"I read the case file at lunch this morning," Ortega says. "Hank Grand's file, from twenty-seven years ago." He hesitates for a moment, his eyes dropping then rising again, his tone gentle. "I know what he did to you."

We're on the road, crawling alongside rush-hour traffic on the Manhattan Bridge. I've already suggested that Ortega use his siren to speed up our journey, but he only chuckled.

"And where would the traffic go?" he told me. "Into the river?"

So now I'm fidgeting in the back seat, wanting to be rid of the cop, the day and our body. I need a vacation. I need respite.

We're halfway across the Brooklyn Bridge when my disposable phone belts out a string of cheery little tones. I dutifully fish it out of my bag. Without phone mail, I don't have a lot of choice.

"Hi, Carolyn, it's Malaya Castro." The cheery tone again, high-pitched, almost girlish. "How are you?"

"How am I?" I laugh and Ortega laughs with me. He hits the siren twice, *whoop, whoop.* "Never better, Malaya. Never better."

"Great." She takes a breath. "I got a call from the review board a few minutes ago. They've scheduled a hearing." When I don't respond, she adds, "On your case."

"When?"

"Friday, ten a.m. You'll have to be there."

"And you?"

"I'll be there, too. You won't be alone."

I glance out the window, staring for a moment at the Staten Island Ferry as it crosses the bay. The wind is up and the orange ferry appears small against the whitecaps. "Why are they doing this? Why now?"

"Kings County is part of the New York City Health and Hospital System. Anything that goes wrong, that catches the attention of the media, reflects on the mayor. The administration's only doing what all administrations do. They're circling the wagons."

"And I'm what? A hostile Indian?"

"We'll find the answer to that one on Friday. Just remember, you need to be there. You need to show them who you are and that you're fully functioning." She hesitates briefly as a horn sounds, then says, "Are you in a car?"

"Yeah, I'm with Detective Ortega. He drove me to the morgue, to identify my father's body."

"Seriously?"

"Yeah, why?"

"Because these days identifications are made at home through the ME's website. There was no need to travel. You've been played."

Dinner isn't much, a can of tuna fish, the last of the mayo, a little red onion, two slices of whole wheat bread. Courtesy of a food pantry run out of a Baptist Church on Bergen Street.

Meager or not, I'm sharing my dinner with Marshal, the man-boy who makes no judgments, who takes us as we are. Marshal came over because he found a new email, which is still unread. He's proud of this discovery but prouder still that a website specializing in electronic music has added one of his compositions to its playlist. He tells me the name of the site, which I forget before the words reach my ears. I've listened to Marshal's compositions and I can't make them any more than noise. Irritating noise at that. But for Marshal, this is the first time he's been recognized by any professional and he's as happy as a five-year-old on his birthday.

Far be it from me to rain on Marshal's dream. I even share the last of a small pound cake, which I was hoping to finish myself. By that time, we're in the living room and Marshal's pulling a joint from his shirt pocket.

"You think the cops are gonna do a search?" He doesn't wait for a reply before adding, "Those notes on the table? If the cops get a search warrant, they're gonna take 'em. So, how about I copy them and stash the copies at my place?"

I nod and smile. "I like it, Marshal. I like you, too."

He blushes, then offers me the joint. "You want some?" he asks.

I don't and I tell him so. Still, I don't object when he lights up. I merely hold out my hand for the email. "Alright, I'm ready now."

Zenia, greetings.

I fear I've become obsessed. When I first learned of Hank Grand's death, I discarded the possibility that my multi had anything to do with the matter. Bear in mind, Hank Grand produced child pornography, regularly dealt with mob figures who distributed his films and passed twenty-seven years in some of New York's most violent prisons. Consider also that Hank Grand stood a bit over six feet tall and weighed nearly 250 pounds. His daughter, by contrast, is of average height and slim—she can't weigh more than 120 pounds—and to my knowledge has never been violent.

Surely, under the circumstances, my dismissing the possibility that Carolyn Grand (or one of her many doppelgangers) murdered her father can be forgiven.

Forgiven or not, my opinion abruptly changed following an interview conducted in my office by a homicide detective named Ortega. He probed as best he could and I did the same. I wanted to learn something of the circumstances surrounding Grand's death, but Ortega was no more forthcoming with me than I with him. Nevertheless, I did come away convinced that my little multi is a legitimate suspect.

Following Ortega's departure, the identity calling herself Eleni (just to remind you, Eleni's the promiscuous identity) arrived for her visit. As this was my first opportunity to examine Eleni, I paid close attention to her appearance and manner. First the obvious. She threw her sexuality in my face, making clear her willingness to give me her body if I wanted it. (I didn't and don't.) Her behavior, when it wasn't teasing, was challenging, and she didn't let up. Still, after I got past her charade, I found something else, something she would have preferred I not find, a hard and cold assessment devoid of empathy.

That got me going, Zenia, and I began to speculate, my thoughts running toward the obsessive. Suppose I reverse engineered my original judgment. Suppose I began by assuming that Carolyn Grand murdered her father. Well, then, instead of a single suspect, I'd have five to consider.

Selena was the first to be discarded. Too unfocused and utterly nonviolent. Victoria came next. Proper, even a bit conceited, she's obsessed with her image. I cannot imagine her committing a murder. Tina presented something of a problem. I've seen her angry, as you know, but her anger, when I examined it, was the anger of a child, a nine-year-old throwing a tantrum.

That left Kirk, Eleni, and Martha. I'll take Martha first. A self-identified lesbian, Martha is relentlessly capable. Her mindset is masculine and she instinctively focuses on resolving problems, the sooner the better. Hank Grand was certainly a problem. Did she resolve it?

Kirk shares Martha's sexual preferences, but considers himself to be a man trapped in a woman's body. In session, he is fearless and makes no effort to placate me. Nevertheless, of all the identities, he seems the least concerned with their shared misfortunes.

I've already described Eleni. I believe Eleni could have played the seductress long enough to put Hank Grand off his guard, to overcome the size disparity. Further, I can imagine her killing him for the pure pleasure of watching him die. She's that cold.

Enough, dear Zenia, lest I become too excited for sleep. It's getting late, and there's nothing to be decided here, lacking as I do, all knowledge of how Grand was killed. Was he stabbed, bludgeoned, shot, poisoned? Are the ladies innocent? Guilty? Just now, that's for them to know and me to find out. And if my expectations are not terribly high, I do believe I'll be royally entertained along the way, which is all I ask. So, good night. Sleep well.

Laurence

CHAPTER THIRTY-ONE
KIRK

Right away, as I come out of the building, I'm drawn to a middle-aged man on the far side of the street. He's leaning against the streetlight and obviously watching our front door. Now he's watching me. I stare back at him for a minute, but he doesn't turn away. One side of his mouth is curved upward, the insolent pose so artificial I want to laugh, even as his dark eyes dart across my body. His thinning hair is cut short and spikes up at odd angles, matching a scruffy beard that runs to his larynx. Pulled tight over a bulging chest, his sweatshirt bears the likeness of a wolf.

I slide my hand into the pocket of my khakis, the feel of the paring knife in its sheath comforting and familiar. If he means to do us harm, he's chosen the wrong Carolyn Grand. I'm not afraid of him, not even a little bit.

Out of nowhere, Martha's voice thrusts itself into my brain, followed by Victoria's. They're talking over each other, but the gist of their demand is plain enough. We've got a hearing tomorrow and our freedom is hanging by a thread. Just go about your business. Better still, turn around, get your dumb ass home and lock the door.

I'm not about to return to that prison they call a home. We're into late September and I plan to enjoy the afternoon, what with New York's street drama in full swing. Unfortunately, we're two days short of our disability check and I'm completely broke, not a penny in my pocket, no rides on the MetroCard. I can't buy a bottle of soda, which means I'll be drinking from a juice bottle filled with tap water stashed in my back pack. It'll be warm by then, warm bleeding into hot, but still a lot more palatable than the dry tuna sandwich. By the time I get to the tuna, it'll be growing fins.

The man across the street folds his arms. He's standing with his back against the streetlight, his feet crossed at the ankles. I stare back at him for another moment, hoping the ladies riding along with me will imprint his features. I'm thinking he's a neighborhood freak, a jerkoff artist in search of inspiration. And maybe a little nearsighted, too, if he's fixated on a man in a woman's body.

I take a right and head off. I'm planning to walk along Flatbush Avenue to the Manhattan Bridge, cross the East River and walk around the Lower East Side. I'm not expecting anything to come of my jaunt, but my access is rare enough to make any time I get enjoyable. Only not today because the man, though he stays on his side of the street, unfolds himself and follows.

Again, I stop and face him directly. This time he appears startled, like he knows something's wrong, but he's not sure what it is. And me, I'm not the brightest star in the sky, because only at that minute do I grasp the obvious. He must know my father. My dead father. In fact, everything, from the stubble on his face to the wolf on his sweatshirt is wrong. The graying stubble is sparse and the wolf shirt would be more suitable on a fifteen-year-old playing street hood. This is a jerk who's learned every lesson in prison, who will always look out of place unless he's wearing a jumpsuit.

Too many conclusions? With no supporting evidence? But I find more evidence in the swell of his biceps and the tree-trunk neck, in his Popeye forearms and his confused expression. Yeah, he's spoken to Hank Grand about his daughter. And without doubt old Hank claimed that his daughter loved every minute, because that's what he told everyone. His little girl was a natural whore. But if that's true, what's up with this dyke who's just standing there, one hand in her pocket, like she's not about to take shit from anybody?

The man reveals more of his street instincts by following when I turn away. He doesn't take shit, either. I know at some point we'll have to confront him, but the prunes have got it right this time. We have to get past the hearing and that means keeping the drama to a minimum. If the review board decides to commit us, we'll be taken into custody on the spot.

And why not? After all, we're crazy.

Well, if the boy can't confront, he can still have a little fun on a pleasant afternoon when he can't afford anything more exciting. I stroll down Lafayette Avenue to Flatbush, then turn toward the waterfront. I take my time, window-shopping at almost every opportunity, including a dog groomer's and an empty check-cashing store. At one point, I take up a position at a bus stop, just another rider peering down Flatbush Avenue. I even glance at my wrist, just as if I had a watch.

But when the bus finally arrives, I walk away.

The jerk has to know I'm playing him by this time. Mocking him, really. Still, he keeps on coming, the way Hank Grand came after his daughter, testing the waters, stubborn and stupid. I lead him to Gold Street, then turn right. Two blocks later, as I pass the Eighty-Fourth Precinct, a uniformed cop, a woman, steps out of a patrol car. I dart across the street, hands raised, doing my best impression of a damsel in distress.

"That man," I say, pointing behind me. "He's been following me since I left my apartment."

The cop, a sergeant, follows my gesture. "Do you know him?" she asks.

"I've never seen him before. But he followed me all the way from South Portland Avenue."

She hesitates for a few seconds as she sizes me up. Maybe thinking I'm too butch to be a damsel. Finally, she nods and says, "Wait here a minute, I'll check him out."

Too late. When I look across the street, the man's turning the corner. He's almost but not quite running, headed toward Flatbush Avenue. The cop follows, in no apparent hurry, and I finally relax when she's out of sight. Now I know something else about the man in the wolf shirt. He's either on parole or has outstanding warrants for his arrest. I'm picking the former.

Five minutes later, the cop returns. She's slightly out of breath, but that look in her pale-green eyes, the tight evaluation, like she's looking into me, not at me, grows more intense.

"He jumped in a cab. He's gone." She hesitates. "You say you never met this man?"

"Never, but he was across the street when I came out."

"And you're afraid of him?"

I smile and shrug, done with the damsel ploy. "Let's just say he was makin' me nervous."

She steps a little closer to me as she reaches into the pocket of her uniform blouse for a business card. "Well, you should be nervous. In your position, I'd be nervous, too. Here, take this. It's got my cell number on it. If you need help, don't hesitate."

I'm wearing a man-tailored white shirt with the sleeves rolled to my elbows. Instead of handing me the card, the cop slides it into my shirt pocket, her fingertips lingering on my breast long enough to make her intentions clear, long enough for me to notice the wedding ring on her finger.

"Maybe," she announces, her eyes boring into mine, "I should give you a ride home. In case that asshole is still in the neighborhood."

"Excellent idea, Sergeant."

"Sheila will do."

"Excellent idea, Sheila. Better safe than sorry."

We take a detour on the way to South Portland Avenue. To a deserted street behind an empty warehouse near the

Gowanus Canal. Sergeant Sheila, as I begin to think of her, maintains a tough-cop attitude. She stares straight ahead as she drives, seeming indifferent. But when I lay my fingertips on the inside of her knee, then slowly draw it along her thigh, her leg trembles and the car lurches forward.

The ice broken, I can't stop touching her. My fingers slide beneath the sleeve of her blouse to stroke the hollow of her armpit, the inside of her elbow, a dimple at the side of her mouth. I trace the curve of an ear and kiss the side of her neck, allowing my breath to wash across her cheek. Then we're parked and in each other's arms, mouths joined.

We stay that way for a long time, lips and tongues dancing, until I drop my mouth to the hollow beneath her chin, my hands to the buttons of her uniform blouse. Sheila has red hair cut short, and her pale skin contrasts sharply with the dark navy of her uniform blouse. I'm imagining her breasts, the milky white of her skin, but I'm still fumbling with the buttons when she pushes my hand away.

I straighten as she unbuckles the belt holding her cop gear: gun, mace, spare magazines, and a folding baton. The wide belt rests on her hips, and she slides it off easily.

"I don't have a lot of time," she tells me as she stuffs belt and hardware into the space between the seat and the door.

I watch her fumble with the zipper on her pants, then slide pants and panties down to her ankles. I don't resist when she draws my left hand down between her legs. I don't protest when she opens my pants, my relaxed-fit jeans, and easily slides her own hand beneath the boxers I'm wearing. It's been a long while since I touched another woman's body and I'm ready to provide whatever she wants. Eyes closed, I give way to my sense of touch, stroking, probing, until she begins to squirm, then to thrash, until she finally grabs my wrist. To slow me down, speed me up? I ignore her, continuing at my own pace until she lays her head against the headrest and her body goes limp.

Only a few minutes later, our clothes in place, I'm asking her to drive me to Flatbush Avenue. As we make our way, seeming to stop at every light, Sheila tells me that she's been transferred. Beginning next week, she'll be working with a vice unit stationed in the North Bronx. As I didn't have any real expectations in the first place, I'm not exactly broken up. One-night stands are the only stands I'm likely to get, me and Eleni, and we're used to it. Still, I nod once and drop my chin, like I give a shit. Like I haven't had better.

I give Sheila a peck on the cheek as I back out of the car. She nods, her smile seeming almost painful. She wants to be rid of me, but I'm not through.

"One question," I say. "The wedding ring?"

"Yeah?"

"A man or a woman?"

"A man."

CHAPTER THIRTY-TWO
VICTORIA

For once, on this our day of judgement, the breaks go our way. First, because I'm inhabiting our body, not Kirk or Eleni. Second, because I gained control early enough to prepare. I'm wearing a pale-green suit, a yellow blouse with a round collar and flesh-colored pantyhose. My nails are trimmed and polished, my makeup fresh and lightly applied, my hair swept across my ears. I've a thin gold chain (plated, of course) around my throat and a ring I picked up at a flea market on my finger. The ring holds a four- or five-carat amber stone that I like to pretend is a citrine, but that's almost surely glass.

No question, we look good today. But my appearance, my presentation, is a sham. Inside, I feel more like a defendant than a professional, a defendant on her way to the courtroom after learning the jury's reached a verdict, yes or no, door A or door B. The heels of my pumps rap against the stone floor with each step I take, marking the distance, closer and closer, our lives, as always, out of our hands.

Chin up, I tell myself. Show fear and the dogs will bite. Stay brave and you have, at least, a chance.

The city's built a new extension with a shiny glass façade on Kings County Hospital. The façade makes the hospital appear new and modern, but once you get into the building the fact that Kings County is 150 years old becomes apparent. I'm walking through an administrative wing, one of the oldest in the complex, toward a conference room near the Accounting Department. Ahead, I see a woman standing in front of an open door. In her twenties, she's short and plump with the bright-yellow hair I associate with teenage Latinas. A black briefcase rests on the floor beside her.

The woman steps toward me as I come closer, her eyes inquisitive. "Carolyn Grand?"

I nod as I take the hand she offers. "Yes, and you're . . . my lawyer."

She ignores the skeptical tone. "You look fantastic. You're beautiful."

"You seem surprised. What exactly were you expecting?"

"I don't know." She cocks her head to the side and grins. "Maybe wild hair spiking in all directions, eyes bulging out of your head. And drool, of course, lots and lots of drool."

I laugh, despite myself. We're crazy, the issue decided long ago by experts. But our illness is not the result of some faulty gene. Our psychosis is reactive and we're never what people who meet us for the first time expect. I find myself wondering how Malaya might have received Martha if she'd walked down that corridor in denim shorts with her hairy legs on display. Or, God help us, Eleni in seven-inch hooker heels.

Malaya reaches for her briefcase and waves me forward. "Shall we go in?"

My heart jumps into my throat as I enter the room, knowing as I do, as we all do, that I might walk back out a ward of the state. Confined, of course, for my own good.

A hush follows my entry, all eyes on me: What will I do? How will I act? Halberstam recognizes me. I can see it in his eyes, see him make a quick calculation. More than likely, he's revising whatever argument he intends to make. One diagnosis for presentable Victoria, another for Martha or Kirk.

I nod to him, the gesture obligatory, before I sit to face the panel. There are five of them seated behind a conference table with a faux-leather top. The administrative law judge, Mitchell Jefferson, sits in the middle, so old, pale and shriveled that he might be his own shroud. Two men and two women sit to his left and right, the women on the right and the men on the left. The two men, both in late middle age, are Dr. Plink and Dr. Scotto. On one level, they seem polar opposites, Plink trim and fit, Scotto ready to order a casket. The man's wheezing with every breath, and his watery eyes are as yellow as my blouse.

The two women are Dr. Ewing and Dr. Vasarian. Vasarian appears to be in her sixties, but Ewing, a black woman, is much younger. She's the only one who looks directly at me and I desperately want to read sympathy in her look. I discover pity instead. We're going down.

I take a deep breath, telling myself: You can deal with this. You've been there before. Sooner or later they have to let you out. Meanwhile, I'm an eyeblink away from bursting into tears.

"All present?" Judge Jefferson doesn't wait for a reply. "Good, then let's get started."

The door opens at that moment and a young man steps into the room. He's got that crazy hair you find on six-year-old boys just out of the shower and a lopsided smile that belies his apology.

"Sorry to interrupt," he says, dropping into a chair set against the wall.

Everybody straightens, even Judge Jefferson, who more or less uncoils. As Malaya explained it, there are thousands of administrative law judges in New York and they're not elected. They're appointed by a chief administrative law judge who may be fired by the mayor at any time for any reason.

Jefferson's voice is a lot stronger when he speaks up, but his smile is the grimace of a lizard under the shadow of a diving hawk.

"Sir, are you in the right room?"

The man unzips his jacket to reveal a placard attached to a chain that circles his neck. I can only read a single word of what's printed on the placard, but I know it's the right word: PRESS.

"This is a public hearing, right?"

Malaya Castro reaches beneath the table to squeeze my hand. And though her eyes remain focused on Judge Jefferson, the message is clear enough. She told us she'd have our backs and she'd meant it. Judge Jefferson looks at the doctors to his left, to his right, and suddenly they're all looking at each other, unspoken questions flying back and forth like bullets. Who, what, how, why? The man with the ultrathin laptop resting on his thighs has all the answers, but he's not talking.

"Well, then," Jefferson says. "We'll begin with Dr. Halberstam. Please read your report, Doctor."

Although Halberstam's notes are laid out on the table, he doesn't intend to consult them. He turns them facedown, then starts to rise, thinks better of it, and drops back into his seat.

"Carolyn Grand was released from involuntary commitment on July 21 of this year. She entered therapy as a condition of her release and I was engaged to conduct that therapy. We've met thirty-four times since then, the last two days ago."

The good doctor stops abruptly. His chin moves to the left, as though he's about to peek over his shoulder, but then he catches himself and takes a breath. Behind him, the reporter's fingers fly across the keyboard: *click, click, click, click*.

"Regarding the death of Carolyn Grand's father, I've inquired, of course, at every session, with the same result each time. On one level, this is unsurprising. As individual identities may be absent for relatively long periods of time, dissociative identity disorder inevitably produces memory loss. On another level, the constant reply 'I didn't exist' to any question regarding Carolyn Grand's movements on the night her father was killed seems artificial. More to the point, it mirrors a pattern of evasion that manifested itself early in therapy and that I have not yet penetrated. Carolyn Grand is extremely guarded and quite intelligent. She intentionally withholds. This is only to be expected, given her childhood experience, but unless there's a breakthrough, the main goal, to integrate her various identities, is very likely to fail."

Halberstam drones on for a moment, excoriating us for our collective failure to trust him, but I find myself drifting away. Now that the record's official, recorded by the court and the media, Halberstam's merely covering his risk-averse butt.

Jefferson waits patiently until Halberstam pauses for a moment, then leans forward. "Your recommendation, Doctor?"

"I recommend, short term, that Carolyn Grand remain in therapy. I would also recommend that her status be reviewed again thirty days from now." He lifts his chin but doesn't look at me. "Assuming, of course, the police take no action."

CHAPTER THIRTY-THREE

VICTORIA

Should I applaud Halberstam's cleverness? It's tempting. He's requesting a sword he can dangle above our necks for the next month, at the very least. I watch him flip his notes over so that the writing faces up and I'm wondering what's written there. I can't help myself. Then Malaya speaks out.

"May I ask the witness a few questions, Your Honor?"

"Go ahead."

"Dr. Halberstam, you initially scheduled Carolyn Grand for five sessions per week. Is that right?"

"Yes."

"A short time later, I don't have the exact date, you reduced the number of sessions to three."

"I did."

Halberstam raises his shoulders, expecting, I think, to be asked why he reduced the number of sessions, but Malaya simply moves on.

"Dr. Halberstam, you referred to the murder of Carolyn Grand's father, Henry Grand. As you raised the issue, I need to ask you a few questions regarding the investigation."

"Fine."

"Tell me, Doctor, have you viewed the crime scene?"

I glance behind me. The reporter's tapping away, a slight smile pulling at the ends of his mouth.

"No."

"Do you know how Mr. Grand was killed?"

"No."

"Do you know where he was killed?"

"No."

"Have you had access to the autopsy results?"

"No."

"Have you reviewed any forensic examinations of trace evidence collected at the scene?"

"No."

"Have you interviewed any witnesses, perhaps at the site of the homicide?"

"No."

"Have the police given you definite reason to believe that Carolyn Grand is a target of their investigation?"

"No."

Malaya finally takes a breath. She looks at Halberstam for a moment, maybe giving him a little credit. Halberstam's tone remained firm and steady throughout when he might easily have become defensive.

"I have no more questions, Doctor. Thank you."

Malaya shifts her focus to Judge Jefferson. I sense a warning in that look or at least a challenge. Jefferson blinks and says, "Do you want to call any witnesses?"

"I believe Dr. Halberstam to be my witness, Your Honor, but I have no one else to call. I do, however, want to speak to the issue at hand. For the record."

Jefferson manages to raise a hand. "Please."

"Okay," Malaya smiles, a thousand-watter that seems, at least from the side, thoroughly genuine. "This is an administrative hearing, not a trial, so I won't bore the panel with legal jargon. My basic argument is simple enough to be reduced to one short sentence: nothing has changed. For example, while she was in this hospital, you determined that Carolyn Grand did not present an immediate danger to herself or to the public. Nothing has changed. You demanded that Carolyn Grand enter therapy as a condition of release, which she immediately did. Nothing has changed. Her therapist kept a close watch on her initially, demanding that she appear every weekday, but then reduced the number of sessions when he, too, decided that she presented no immediate danger to herself or to the public. Nothing has changed. Carolyn Grand has been living independently for ten years, paying her rent, maintaining her household, cooking, cleaning, taking long walks in one or another of the city's parks. Nothing has changed. The incident that brought Carolyn Grand to your attention was unfortunate but not illegal, and you factored that incident into your decision to release her. Nothing has changed. Henry Grand, Carolyn's father, was murdered shortly after being released from prison. The police are still investigating, but there's nothing to indicate that Carolyn Grand is a suspect, not a scintilla of actual evidence. She was and remains Henry Grand's victim. Nothing has changed."

It's over. The review board's accepted Halberstam's recommendation, perhaps, as Malaya explained, to shift the blame should I be arrested. But we're out for the next thirty days and I feel like I'm standing two feet above the floor. Call it a Serena moment, like someone reinvented the world with me at the center. I can't help myself. I put my arms around Malaya and then we're hugging and hopping. Dignity be damned.

"Who was that guy?" I finally ask.

"His name is Mitch Yerewin."

"Is he really a journalist?"

"Yeah, he's credentialed by the city. Mitch does podcasts for a site called SimmeringCity. It's very insider, but he does okay. He did an interview with a male escort that got thirty thousand listens."

"A male escort?"

"The man described himself as a thirty-year-old pool boy." Malaya hesitates for a moment as we step away from each other. "Bureaucrats," she tells me, "hate to be looked at. They want to operate in darkness whenever possible. Jefferson didn't know exactly who Mitch was, only that some other bureaucrat issued his credentials and there was no way to get him out of there. You might think about that as you go forward. I noticed Halberstam turn over his notes when Mitch arrived. I don't know what he might have said, but I can't bring myself to believe it would have been beneficial. So take notes as you go along, lock him in." She gives my hand a final squeeze. "And most of all, don't talk to the cops. Remember, I'm not your attorney. I'm court appointed to represent you in front of the review board. But if the cops pick you up, call me and I'll get them off your back."

CHAPTER THIRTY-FOUR

MARTHA

Three days since the review board cut us loose and we've descended into chaos. Driven there by memories better left forgotten. Memories that I *had* forgotten. No more. Now I feel every pain, every degradation. They come at me in bits and pieces, all the more powerful for being long suppressed. At times, I can hear Carolyn Grand screaming.

So, it's not just Tina. It's all of us as we come and go, as we're shoved into the front ranks. Until we prefer oblivion to existence.

Who's to understand this? Who's to fix what's wrong with us? Who's to protect us? Halberstam? There's no one to call. No lover to offer a comforting hand, no parent or friend, not even each other. Because when it hurts bad enough you think only of escaping your own pain. Better them than you.

I must be exaggerating because a casual observer would have to conclude that we've drawn closer together. The memos on the table prove it. Before Eleni propositioned the cop and our father was released, before Halberstam and Kings

County Hospital, before Judge Jefferson and his review board, we almost never cooperated. We schemed instead, our dysfunctional family dedicated to assassination. We plotted to kill each other off.

We're past that now and our alliances have shifted. When I'm not around, I want Kirk or Eleni to run the body. I want someone tough in place, ready to go. The threat might come from the cops or from the man who followed Kirk. He's taken up his station by the streetlight for the past two days. Chain-smoking cigarettes and spitting into the street. Yesterday, he showed up in a sleeveless T-shirt, his tattoo-covered arms fully revealed. I couldn't make out the tattoos, but I imagined them to be devils and skulls and broken women. The markings of a dangerous moron.

I walk over to the window and peer out across the street. He's not there, but I suddenly realize that he reminds me of someone.

The Acevedas had three foster children, including me. They were all girls and old enough by then to make a run for it if they got a chance. Where they'd go—except onto the street where life would be even harder—was anyone's guess. But our foster parents took precautions anyway. When they were off to some family function, they'd leave Uncle Esteban to mind the store. Uncle Esteban was short and very thick. He was a man not of few words but of no words. He never touched us, although I can't imagine Benny or Angela objecting. He didn't talk to us, either, and his routine never varied. The first thing he'd do was angle the television. Then he'd fetch a chair from the kitchen and set it against the door. Finally, he'd wait, expressionless, for his patrons to come home.

When Carolyn Grand first entered the Acevedas' apartment in the Bronx, there was one of her. When she left, four years later, there were nine and the family was growing. And nothing she discovered in her assigned group home, or at school when she was finally allowed to go again, slowed that process.

The knock on the door comes at 10:30 a.m., as I'm scrubbing the bathtub. I'm hoping it's Marshal or even Doyle, but it's the two detectives, Greco and Ortega. They're accompanied by three uniformed cops with CSU patches on their shirts, one a female. All five wear blue latex gloves, including Greco, who hands me several printed pages.

"Search warrant," he announces. "Step back."

He doesn't wait for me to respond. He pushes past me, starting a little parade. The three uniformed cops first, then Ortega. I'm seriously pissed and I make sure I get a good look at Ortega's face. His mouth is tight, his nostrils flaring as he draws breath. I think he wants to say something, but he doesn't meet my eyes as he passes. I understand. Yeah, he read Hank Grand's file. Sure, he knows what Daddy did to us. But he'll do his job anyway.

I back into the apartment and close the door. The uniformed cops are already at work, Ortega, too. Only Greco remains idle. He's standing in the center of our living room, staring at me with tiny blue eyes so bright they seem to glow. I don't know what he wants and I really don't give a shit. One of the uniformed cops tosses the cushions off the couch. Now he's running his fingers between the back and the seat, looking, perhaps, for lost change.

"Miss Grand?" Greco says when it's obvious I won't be the first to speak.

I'm still not answering. Mostly because I'm afraid of what might come out of my mouth. A few feet away, my couch is tipped onto its knees and the backing ripped off the underside. This furniture, crappy as it may be, is all we have. I want to smash the cops. I want to smash all of them. But they're grown men, large men at that, with guns at their sides.

I feel myself shrinking. As if we weren't small enough already. As if we weren't already helpless.

"Miss Grand?"

"What?"

"The warrant includes your cell phone. If you'll show me where it is . . ."

"We don't have a cell phone. We used up the minutes on the last one and I tossed it about a week ago."

Greco looks like he wants to say something but doesn't know what it is. If we had a cell phone, of course, he could use its GPS to track our movements. But our cell went the way of our many burner phones shortly after my visit to the morgue. We'll replace it when we have the money. For now, the house phone will have to do.

Behind Greco, I watch Ortega approach the cop who turned over our couch. He taps him on the shoulder and says, "Keep it neat." Ortega's voice is low, nearly muffled, as if he were speaking against some restraint. The cop looks up at Ortega in apparent surprise.

"*Por favor*, Carlos. Tell your buddies."

My first thought, given my trip to the morgue, is good cop/bad cop. Greco plays the bully; Ortega plays the pal. He plays the concerned parent we never had. Nevertheless, I'm pleased when Carlos rises to feet and trots into the kitchen.

"When was the last time you had a cell phone?" Greco asks.

I finally look down at the papers in my hand. What I have is a search warrant not an arrest warrant. There's even a list of items to be recovered: knives, stained clothing, cell phones, computers and a DNA sample.

"I asked you a question. When did you last have a cell phone?"

I watch Ortega rifle through the memos on our table. The note from our father, the one with the address of the hotel is long gone, of course. Finally, I make myself clear. "Fuck off, detective. I've got nothing to say to you."

Greco shakes his head and smiles. "That's not nice, Miss Grand. In fact, if I had to guess, I'd say you weren't raised right."

Forty-five minutes later, they're gone. Leaving me with a sore cheek on the inside where the female cop dragged the DNA swab, and a list of the items they've seized. The list includes our barely functioning computer, our memos (already copied by Marshal), our one decent chef's knife, and a dozen bags containing various garments. Still, they've been neat and I suppose I should be grateful. They've emptied the cupboards and the closets, piling pots, pans, cutlery, and food on any available surface. Nothing on the floor. Very considerate.

I can't stand mess and I go to work right after I lock the door. As I rearrange the shelves in the kitchen, I'm again seized by the poverty of our life. Then a memory rises. My father is sitting in the living room, eyes glued to the television. He has a cigarette in one hand and a bottle of orange soda in the other. I'm crossing the room, headed for the kitchen and a glass of water. As I pass the side of the chair, his hand shoots out, quick as a snake, and he grinds the cigarette into my belly. Why? Because Carolyn Grand has a urinary tract infection and can't fuck Cousin Mike.

This is how we marked the days of our lives.

This is how we marked the days of our lives and still we survive.

CHAPTER THIRTY-FIVE

KIRK

There's blood in the water and our shithead of a therapist can smell it. He's leaning over his desk, his gaze intent and questioning. Something's different? What is it? Can I exploit this development?

Search warrants aren't signed by judges because they like cops and want to be nice to them. The cops have to write an affidavit demonstrating probable cause to find whatever's listed on the warrant. Probable cause boils down to evidence of some kind, which the cops obviously have on us. And now, sitting in the submissive seat across from our caring therapist, I can't say that we didn't do it. I can only claim that I, myself, didn't kill our father. But why would anyone believe me? After all, if we did bump off dear old Dad, at least one of us must be lying about it because we've all claimed innocence.

As I watch Halberstam open the center drawer of his desk and reach in for his favorite prop, I'm suddenly reminded of a quote from Benjamin Franklin. Something about hanging separately if we don't hang together. Of course, we won't hang, separately or together. But we'll definitely share the same cell, whether or not I wielded the knife that killed my father. And the murder weapon must have been a knife because the cops seized one of ours and knives were specified in the warrant. I know this because Martha's memo was quite detailed.

Halberstam points a finger in my direction. "Are you alone, Kirk?" he asks me. "Or are others lurking?"

I take a second to check but sense no other presence, which doesn't mean there's no one there.

"Not that I can tell."

"Good, because I want to work on something today. Tell me. Did you hate your father?"

"Probably."

"Probably?"

I take a breath and shrug. "You gotta hate the asshole, right? Given what he did? But I can't say I spent all that much time thinking about him, at least before he showed up."

"What about Carolyn?"

"What about her?"

"Did Carolyn, as a child, hate her father?"

"How would I know?" I don't want to remember a single second of Carolyn's life with Daddy and I change the subject before Halberstam gets up a head of steam. "At the hearing, Doctor, you told the board that you didn't know who was in control of Carolyn's body on the night my father was snuffed. Now I'm telling you. Martha was in control. She spent the evening at home watching TV."

"How do you know this? Were you there?"

"We write memos, Doctor." And thank God that Marshal had thought to copy ours. "Martha . . ."

Halberstam waves me off. "I'll need to see the memos, of course."

"I can only promise they'll be produced if I'm around for the next session."

"Ah, the great disclaimer. Don't blame me if Victoria shows up without the memos because I'm not in control. I hear one or another version of this excuse at every session. But here's the thing, Kirk. Therapy can't succeed unless patients take responsibility. You tell me you want to gain control, to unify, but then, at every opportunity, you employ your . . . your separateness to excuse your failures. You're on a merry-go-round, all of you, and you need to get off."

In fact, I have no desire to get off. The only thing I really want is more rides. I encourage Halberstam with a nod, but he's not finished.

"Consider this," he announces. "You told me that you write memos in order to keep each other abreast. Couldn't you, Kirk, when you get home, write a memo reminding the others to bring all the memos to our next session? Instead, you offer the standard disclaimer."

I have to laugh. Halberstam just kicked my ass and there's no wriggling off the hook. I shot off my big mouth and now we'll have to produce the memos. In fact, if Serena's around to do the writing, or Victoria, we'll write a few new ones to replace the ones we leave behind.

"You're right," I admit. "I think you're gonna be bored reading them, but we'll get them here."

CHAPTER THIRTY-SIX
ELENI

He's outside, the man with the tattoos. The one who frightens everyone but Kirk. I'm pissed because I've been thinking about Ortega and the sight of this jerk cut through my best fantasy like a lightning bolt through a paper kite. What I'm not, though I'm about to leave, is afraid.

I'm wearing a pair of Victoria's slacks and a pearl-gray sweater with a high neck. Reasonably demure but suitable to the task at hand. I slip into a light jacket, check my shoulder bag for the canister of pepper spray and head out the door. I won't be a prisoner, not until they put us in handcuffs. And even then, I'm hoping the cops are horny enough to corrupt. One last fling in the back seat of a cruiser before the cell door clangs shut.

Martha was around earlier. She urged me to take matters seriously. She insisted that we're under siege, threats coming from all directions, doom, doom, and more doom. So what?

I didn't kill my father. I'm innocent and I know that in America innocence will protect me. Just like it's always protected me.

So, I'm horny and I'm pissed, at my father, at that sick asshole who calls himself a doctor, at the cops and their bullshit search warrant. And the guy across the street? The guy with the bowling-ball arms and tree-trunk neck? The way I'm thinking, he's the perfect outlet for the pissed half of the equation. As for the other half, the Ortega part, I've decided to put that aside for the present. I've got another mission in mind. I intend to visit the Golden Inn Hotel.

I've been to the Golden Inn a few times. Not as a hooker but as a matter of convenience. Somehow, the debased ambiance—the gray sheets, the stained floors, the mingled odors of sex and disinfectant—turned me on. My lovers on those occasions were sailors in town for Fleet Week, sailors just off the boat after weeks at sea. One mistook me for a hooker when I hit on him in a local dive. I didn't take his money, but . . .

But for once, I'm not out to get laid.

I wasn't inside the hotel on the night Hank Grand was killed. But if one of the others was, I want to know. There's another incentive as well. I'm hoping to see the room where that scumbag died. I don't know who killed him, but I want to believe that one of us did. I want to believe we killed our daddy in cold blood. That way I can imagine him in pain, begging for life, knowing, as he bleeds to death, that his little girl isn't little anymore.

I'm not really afraid of prison. Our looney-tunes bona fides are proven beyond a reasonable doubt and no sane prosecutor will bring us to trial. Instead, we'll be shipped off to one or another of New York's psychiatric hospitals, assigned most likely to a unit for the criminally insane.

With luck, we could be released in as few as ten years.

What do you do if you feel like you're going insane and you're already insane? I walk through the door, eager for conflict. The man across the road straightens, then comes right at me. I don't turn a hair, don't change expression, the only moving part my thumb, which finds its way to a button at the top of the pepper spray canister.

Angry males? Been there, done that. Often enough to learn the only relevant lesson. Strike first, strike hard, get your ass in the wind.

But it doesn't happen. He comes to a stop ten feet away, his gaze now suspicious. I'm not running off and I'm not showing fear and I don't look like Kirk. Not exactly.

"You," he says. "I know what you did."

I'm thinking I should cut him off, but I can't stop myself from wanting to know what he has to say. Given all the circumstances, he can only be talking about Hank Grand's murder. I hold my ground but remain silent.

"Not talkin'?" He looks at me for a moment before realizing that he's answered his own question. Finally, almost desperately, he blurts it out. "The cops are tryin' to put it on me. But you were there. I seen you were there."

"Then you must've been there yourself."

"So fuckin' what? Me and your old man were friends. I had no reason—"

I cut him off. "You were there for what exactly, you and my daddy?"

"I don't have to explain myself." His eyes narrow and I know he wants to deal with his frustrations by smashing whatever's in front of him. "Hank told me you was comin' for a visit."

"At the Golden Inn?" When he doesn't reply, I lose it for a moment. "So, tell me, asshole, how was it supposed to be? Were you gonna share me? Two on one? One at a time? How did you have it figured?"

"It wasn't that way at all. I was in a different room with a hooker." He takes a step toward me, then stops. "What your father done ain't my business, lady. I know you was there."

"Have I got this right? You were inside a room with a prostitute, but you were also outside and saw me? Cut the crap, man. If the cops suspect you, it's probably because you killed him. You killed him and now you're lookin' for a patsy. Well, I'm not buying, so fuck off."

He closes his eyes for a second, as if he can't believe what he's hearing. I watch his hands curl into fists, watch the cords on his neck bulge. I know what's likely to come next and I slide the canister of pepper spray out of my bag. I can hear Victoria now, moaning in despair. Crazy Eleni, destructive Eleni, worthless, useless. I don't give a damn. I'm about to empty the canister down the asshole's throat, let him spend the next week in the hospital with his lungs on fire.

But it's not happening, not today. His shoulders slump as he draws a breath and steps back. "This ain't over," he tells me.

I want the last word and I search for a snappy comeback. Too late. He turns and heads back the way he came. I watch him cross the street before I return the pepper spray to my bag. Then I'm on my way, wishing that somewhere along the line I'd learned to whistle.

CHAPTER THIRTY-SEVEN
ELENI

The Golden Inn doesn't come within a mile of living up to its name. It's an isolated, four-story tenement converted into single rooms. Totally out of place in an industrial neighborhood. Still, it serves its purposes, luring the few hookers who still work beneath the elevated highway on Fourth Avenue. The whole of South Brooklyn is rapidly gentrifying and the working girls will soon be gone, along with the bodegas, the check-cashing joints and the payday lenders. The Golden Inn will be gone as well, probably converted into million-dollar condos.

The inn hangs on for now, though in midafternoon on a workday it's practically deserted. I march through the front door, then toward a small, bullet-proof cubicle where the desk clerk sits. He's just as I remember him, a tired old man who's lived his life in a tarnished corner of the world. His eyes are ancient. They seem to look in rather than out.

He examines me carefully as I approach. I don't see a glimmer of recognition, but his eyes brighten when I hold up a twenty. "I'm a reporter," I tell him. "Checking into the murder of a man named Henry Grand."

"Yeah, last week. Not the first this year, by the way." His voice is indistinct, as if he's speaking through a wad of phlegm. Which, given the full ashtray on his desk, seems likely. "OK, tell me what ya want from me?"

"Well, for starters, were you on duty the night he was killed?"

"Yeah, I was."

I take a step closer and pass the twenty through the slot, but he still doesn't recognize me. Does that mean we weren't here?

"Can I get into his room?" I ask.

"That's Room 307. Cops have it sealed off. They got the key, too."

"What about the room next to 307? Is there a connecting door?"

"Yeah, but it's probably locked on the other side."

"Do you mind if I check it out?"

He glances behind him, discovers the key for 309 on its hook. "You ain't gonna take someone up there?"

"Are you kidding?" I step back and raise my elbows, he better to display an outfit I chose because there's nothing about it that says hooker. The demonstration brings a smile to his face, revealing missing teeth on both sides of his mouth.

"Name's Tom Randall. With two *l*'s." He slips the key hrough the slot. "You decide to use my name in the papers, spell it right."

Beyond the front desk, the Golden Inn is a series of stacked corridors broken by an elevator and a stairwell. I don't bother with the elevator. I climb the narrow stairway, passing a middle-aged hooker and her teenage client on the way. At the third-floor landing, about halfway down the corridor to my right, two strips of yellow, crime-scene tape form an X across one of the doors. It's Hank Grand's death chamber and I'm drawn to it, the pull irresistible.

A few seconds later, I'm facing the door wondering if I should try the handle, when a hand closes on my right forearm. Closes hard.

"Hey, baby, you up for a date?"

I turn and try to shake my arm free. No dice. He's tall and fat and smells of recent sex. He's also drunk enough to be totally obnoxious but not drunk enough to fall over. I look up and down the empty hall. Nothing there.

"Let go of me."

"What, my money's not good enough? Gimme a break." His tongue flashes across his already-wet lips. "Half-and-half. How much?"

"I'm not a prostitute." My purse is hanging near my right hip and there's no way I can reach the canister inside while he's holding my arm. I tell myself to calm down. I'm not about to let this jerk get me in a room behind a locked door. I'll scream if it comes to that. But I could still take a beating.

"That's right, you're not a prostitute. You're a whore." His left hand comes up. There's a fifty-dollar bill between his thumb and his forefinger. "Like, if you're not a whore, what the fuck are you doin' inside the hotel?"

His eyes travel across my body as he searches for a place to put the fifty. I'm not wearing a skirt and my sweater rises to my throat, but the man's just drunk enough to come up with a solution. He tries to push the bill into my mouth. Now I'm thinking I have only one chance here. I'm going to turn into him, drive my knee into his crotch, and jerk my arm away. One move, real, real fast. If I succeed, I'll run.

I'm staring up at the john, at the sneer on his face. I'm thinking, *He wants you to resist. He wants to hurt you.* Then the door to Hank Grand's death chamber opens and the cop, Detective Ortega, ducks under the tape. He evaluates the scene in an instant, including the intensity of the man's grip and the relief on my face. Then he flips his jacket open to reveal a gold badge, the badge of a detective, attached to his belt.

"What's going on here?" His eyes bore into mine, the beginnings of a tiny smile just touching the corners of his mouth. My belly tightens and I raise my chin. I want him at that moment as much as I've wanted any of the men who've flitted in and out of my life. Not least because his eyes are on fire.

"This guy solicited me, Officer," I say.

"He did what?"

"He solicited me. And I never saw him before in my life."

The man's already let go of my arm. Now he speaks. "I never touched her."

"Soliciting isn't touching," Ortega says. "Though you were definitely touching her when I opened the door. So, Miss, what did he actually say?"

We're in each other's heads now, whirling around, playful as kittens. "He offered me fifty dollars for half-and-half. I always thought half-and-half was something you find in the refrigerator."

"And look," Ortega points. "There's the fifty dollars between his fingers." He shakes his head. "Know what? I could be mistaken, but it looks like he was trying to shove that bill into your mouth."

"Before he shoved in something else." I put my hand on my hips. "And I'm a respectable woman."

Ortega jerks his chin at the man, who hastily slips the fifty into his pocket. "Take off, jerk. Right now."

A quick learner, the man heads for the stairs, weaving a bit. I start to speak, but Ortega holds up a hand. A minute later, as his head disappears, the man yells out, "Fuck you!"

We laugh, the both of us, but only for a few seconds. Then we're in each other's arms, our mouths joined, the two of us equally heedless. Consequences are for later. Consequences be damned.

"Wow." He allows his hand to linger on the side of my face for a few beats, then drops it to his side. "What's your name?" he asks.

"You don't recognize me?"

"Oh, yes, I recognize you. I just want to know the name you call yourself."

"Eleni."

"And the woman I took to the morgue? Her name is Martha, right?"

"Do you mean the woman you took to the morgue when you could have done the ID in our apartment using the medical examiner's website?"

His face reddens, the skin above his cheeks turning the color of polished mahogany. But he doesn't apologize. "And the woman I met first, on the sidewalk outside your building?"

"Serena."

"And the first time? When Greco and I notified you of your father's death?"

"Kirk. He's a boy."

His laughter is without derision. It continues on for a moment, until he says, "May I kiss you again?"

Slower this time, slower and deeper and so confident in my response, in his. This is a road we haven't traveled and the outcome is entirely unknown. As for me, the idea that someone could know who we are and still want me is one I've refused to entertain.

He steps back. "Why did you come here?"

"I wanted to see the room where my father died."

"Why?"

"Since when do crazy people need reasons?"

I laugh and he joins me. "Well, there's nothing to see." He reaches behind him, turns the knob, and pushes the door open. "The bed and the bedding have been taken into evidence, but you're welcome to look."

He's right. Except for a small table and a chair, the room's empty. No bloodstains anywhere, on the floor or the walls.

"I came to do a final check," he explains. "We're turning the room back to the hotel this afternoon."

"Did you find anything?"

"No, not today."

Neither of us speaks or moves for a moment. But there's nothing awkward about the pause. The outcome's not in doubt. I can see that in his eyes, as I'm sure he can see it in mine. I finally reach out to run the flat of my right hand, gently, from his chest to his waist. His flesh is unyielding, but the smile that lights his face can't be faked. He takes my hand and brings it to his mouth. My whole body's on fire by this time. My crotch is near to molten.

He lowers my hand but doesn't let go. Still, his touch is gentle and I know I can pull away if I want to. I know he's giving me a final choice.

"Shall we?" he asks.

"We shall."

On our way to the stairs, we pass an empty room and duck inside, clothes flying in all directions. I've always believed that the size of women relative to men is one of the great cosmic injustices. Especially because it's one of those always-was-and-always-will-be situations. It can't be remedied and there's no escape. Yet that resentment inevitably vanishes when I hold a man in my arms like I'm holding Bobby Ortega. All in an instant, as if the outrage had been felt by someone else, probably Martha. Now I want to feel Bobby's strength as I dig my fingers into the bunched muscles of his shoulders, as I grip the backs of his arms. I want to be overwhelmed without being forced. Which is exactly the way I feel when Bobby lifts me and lays me on the bed, when I drape my arms across his back, when his mouth drops to mine.

I'd be hard put to name a sexual act I haven't performed at one time or another, but I know a kiss to be more intimate than any joining of body parts. I'm thinking that Bobby knows it, too. Like he knows who we are, what we are. Like he knows that the woman holding his cock isn't even a whole person but some fragment of a deranged freak's imagination. He knows, and he doesn't care.

Bobby's first kisses are tender, almost kind, deepening only as my body responds. "What a woman you are," he tells me. "What a woman you are."

And me, fool that I am, I believe him. And I don't resent his craziness being crotch centered. No, right now I don't resent anything, not even the near certainty that I'll be replaced before dawn. I raise my hips, an invitation he readily accepts. I whisper the words I know he wants to hear.

"Fuck me, Bobby. Fuck me now."

He slides one arm beneath my lower back, the other beneath my shoulders. Then he rises to his knees, taking me with him. I can feel my brain shutting down, a flush building in my face and throat, and I know I'm going to take Bobby home tonight. Fuck the rules. Fuck Martha and her gray world. I want, just this one time, to lie in my own bed with a man in my arms. I don't care if he arrests me tomorrow.

CHAPTER THIRTY-EIGHT

MARTHA

I wake up on the edge of the mattress, staring at a crack in the wall. I'm usually quick out of bed, but I can't seem to get my body moving. My brain, either. Numb is too strong. I'm not numb, just desensitized. I'm drifting and not caring, my eyes glued to the same crack that's been there since we moved in.

Sound returns first, a siren outside my window, Sarah Bennet's dog barking in the apartment upstairs, the elevator rattling. And something else, something I can't quite identify. Something familiar yet utterly strange. I struggle for a few minutes, until my sense of smell kicks in. Then I know but still can't accept the obvious, incredible truth.

There's a man in my bed. A man. In my *fucking* bed.

And I'm naked, not even panties. And the bureau's on the other side of the room. And I feel him stir beside me.

"Eleni?"

I leap out of bed as though launched from a silo. I want to fly into the bathroom where there's at least a towel even if the lock doesn't work. But the damn bed is so close to the wall I have to inch my way down to the foot. All the while knowing, as I know that every demon in hell joined in a round of applause at our birth, that the bastard's eyes are glued to my ass.

I close the bathroom door and lean against it, my ear pressed to the wood. There's no sound of pursuit, no follow-up to his saying Eleni's name. Now what?

Now I realize that I reek of whatever games Eleni played last night. I find myself vowing to kill the bitch even if it means killing myself at the same time. I turn on the shower and jump in without giving the water time to heat. The blast that hits my body is so cold I want to scream. If I do, of course, Eleni's boyfriend will come running to the rescue. I fold my arms over my chest and suck down a breath until the water finally warms.

I calm slowly as I scrub away. Until I'm able to admit that the flesh I inhabit will never be my own. It's rent-a-body, a low-end lease on a few hours of life. Eleni shouldn't have brought anyone home. She's never done it before and there's no forgiving her now. But it's done, in the past, and the clock only turns in one direction. I not only have to get this ass-hole out of our house, I have to convince him that he's not welcome to return.

I turn off the shower and sit on the rim of the tub for a moment. I'm starting to think that I don't give a damn. Everything's crazy now and our shitty lives are falling apart. I don't have the patience for gentle persuasion, so why not give in to the rage we all, even Tina, fight so hard to contain? There's a metal candlestick with a heavy base on the bureau. If necessary . . .

When I finally open the bathroom door a few inches, I find our bedroom empty and the door on the other side of the room closed. A trick? To lure me out in the open? I'd laugh if the possibility didn't parallel many of the games our daddy played with us. But there's no choice here. Whoever was in my bed is in the kitchen now. Frying bacon, which I smell as I leave the bathroom. Bacon is a rare treat for us and we never have it in the house. That means Eleni's lover bought it, which also means that he intended to stay the night. As the bitch surely knew.

Somehow, I'm not surprised to find Detective Ortega by the stove, irresistible Detective Ortega, at least to poor Eleni. Ortega's a good-looking man. It's undeniable. Perhaps forty years old, he's strongly built and confident enough to be charismatic. But he's also a cop who's tricked us once already. I know Eleni and some of the others believe we'll never be sent to a prison. But as far as I'm concerned, this is a distinction without a difference. Units in psychiatric hospitals set aside for the criminally insane are as violent as any housing area in any penal institution. As violent, but far more unpredictable.

Ortega glances over his shoulder. His gaze is a little too intense for his ready smile. "Martha?"

"Good guess, detective. Now what?"

"Look, I'm sorry about this morning. I fell asleep. It won't happen again."

"Bullshit. You bought the groceries last night. You meant to stay."

He looks at me for a moment, then asks, "So, how do you like your eggs?"

Our little table is already set and there's a plate of English muffins, toasted and buttered, in the center. As I slip a muffin onto my plate, Ortega sets a mug of coffee beside me.

"My old man," he tells me, "ran a lunch wagon, back when the Brooklyn waterfront was still industrial. On weekdays, he opened at six in the morning and closed at six at night. He also put me behind the grill when I was ten years old. Summers, Christmas vacation, spring vacation. I'd stand on a wooden milk crate and cook. So, how do you like your eggs?"

I know I'm being seduced, but I don't care. That's because, after all the years in therapy, I'm not seducible. I shift my focus to what Ortega might know about the investigation. What he might know and what he might reveal.

"How 'bout a cheddar omelet?" he asks. "My specialty."

"Fine."

The cop turns and busies himself. He strips the bacon from the pan and lays the slices on a dish towel (clean, if I remember right). Then he drops a chunk of butter into a second pan, whisks four eggs in a bowl, pours the whisked eggs onto the melted butter. While the eggs solidify, he grates the cheese.

I admire precision, the efficient use of any resource, including my own labor. You can accomplish far more if you organize your day than if you let the day happen to you. This is a principle that doesn't interest Eleni or Serena. And why should it when they contribute nothing to the welfare of our household?

Ortega slides the bacon onto a plate and carries it over. A minute later, he lays the omelet in front of me. "There ya go."

The omelet's beautifully cooked, the cheese runny, the bacon crisp. Not exactly haute cuisine, but exotic enough for a body that usually breakfasts on bulk granola. I'm working on the last English muffin when Ortega finally speaks.

"Know what? Me driving you to the morgue wasn't what you think it was."

"Do tell."

His thin smile seems more or less obligatory. "First, I was strongly attracted to Eleni, still am. She's an amazing woman, totally fearless. As for the formal identification of the body, I admit to using it as a pretext." His smile widens. "You know, to see her again. I never thought for a minute that she wouldn't be there when I returned in the afternoon."

"Gimme a break, detective. You could have done the ID the first time you met Eleni."

"Maybe I wanted to spend a little time with her."

"That much is obvious." I slide my plate into the middle of the table and take up the blue mug that holds my now-tepid coffee.

"I did play you," Ortega finally admits. "To an extent. So, how about I try to make it up? Ask me any question. If I can't answer, I'll say so. Otherwise, I'll be honest."

"Cross your heart and hope to die?"

He laughs and I find myself liking him, even though I'm sure liking is the very emotion he wants to evoke. "Go ahead," he tells me.

"Are we suspects?"

"We searched your home, Martha. A judge signed off on the warrant." He shakes his head. "You shouldn't be asking that question."

"Tell me how my father was killed."

"He was stabbed, which you already know because we confiscated your knives when we executed the warrant."

"I'm asking for details. I want to know what happened in that room and when it happened."

Ortega lays his hand on the table and takes up that sincere expression he's so good at. "I can't go there. Crime scene details are always used strategically, mostly during interrogations. For example, we use them to verify confessions or to lure suspects into lying. Remember, *anything* you say can be used against you. What we never do, on the other hand, is casually share those details with a suspect. Now, I don't think much of my partner, in general or as an investigator, but he's the lead on the case and I'm not willing to cut his legs out from under him. Ask me anything else."

"Fine, I will." It's not fine, but I'm looking into his eyes and he's not flinching. He won't be moved. "Are there any other suspects?"

"Many others. Let's start with a paroled con who lived with your father at the Kirkland Housing Facility in the Bronx. The Mott Haven section to be more exact. His name's Alfred O'Neill."

I lean toward the cop. "Let me guess. About five, ten, two hundred pounds, tree-trunk neck, bowling-ball arms, jailhouse tattoos that reach his ears."

"You know him?"

"He was around here the other day." I continue before Ortega reacts, but I'm sure he observed my little pause. There's something we don't want him to know. "Why is O'Neill a suspect?"

"He was at the Golden Inn that night, in the room with the victim at one point. He lied about it at first, but after we confronted him with his prints, which we found in several places, he admitted to being in the room before Grand was killed. The way he tells it, he and your father went there almost every night."

"Why?"

"The answer to that question came from the hookers who use the hotel. O'Neill and Grand were dealing opiates, including heroin. They had an arrangement with the desk clerk and worked out of the same room every night. The odd part is that they didn't use drugs themselves because they were subject to random drug testing at the shelter. So, our working theory, as far as it concerns O'Neill, is that he and his partner got into a dispute over business and O'Neill took him out. That's bolstered by a pair of hookers who heard them arguing over money on several earlier occasions. Partners or not, the two men did not get along."

I get up and clear the table, carrying the dishes to the sink. I can't bring myself to ask the obvious question. And us, what do you have on us? I pour the bacon fat into an empty pickle jar. Later I'll use it to fry up collard greens and white beans, greens and beans, an alternative to the rice we . . . Finally, I blurt it out.

"And what about Carolyn Grand? Is there any reason, besides what you told me before, that she's a suspect?"

"O'Neill claims that he saw you there, but his ID doesn't mean much. He didn't mention seeing you the first time we interviewed him or the second time. Plus, O'Neill's a suspect and he's got every reason to lie. In fact, he gave us three other suspects, two pimps and a paroled con who stays at the shelter, before he named you. No, your problem, so far, is a second ID, this one made by a hooker named Josie Sanchez. Josie's a heroin addict with a long record of solicitation and drug possession arrests. She was stoned when we interviewed her and most likely stoned the night she claimed to see someone who looked like Carolyn Grand, but different somehow. As different, perhaps, as you and Eleni."

I rinse the frying pan and lay it in the drain basket. "What does all that mean? Are we suspects or not?"

"It means that you're near the bottom of a long list of suspects that includes every hooker and pimp who used the hotel. But the real hurdle is still out there. CSU recovered substantial organic material at the murder scene and from your apartment. The DNA is being analyzed and will eventually be cross-compared to yours, your father's, O'Neill's, and the other suspects'. Take this to the bank, Martha. If my partner can put you in that room, he'll arrest you."

"If you do that, we'll be committed to a psychiatric hospital, even if we're never convicted."

Ortega raises a finger. "Greco does not give a shit. He's bucking for detective, first class, and closing cases is how you get there." He stops for a moment, his gaze intent. "But if you don't mind, I have a question. You told me that you were . . . I don't know the right word here."

"In control."

"Okay, you were in control the night your father was killed. You watched TV, went to bed and woke up still in control. I want to know if it's possible that some other self gained temporary control while you slept? Without you knowing it."

"It's possible, yes. But it's also possible that I'm lying through my teeth." As I watch him rise and head for the door, I fire off a pair of questions, my tone now angry. "Why are you doing this? Why are you helping us?"

"You mean, outside of my attraction to Eleni?"

"Yeah."

He opens the door, smiles and shrugs, even as his eyes sadden. "Forget about reasons, Martha. I'm way past reasons. I have been for a long time."

CHAPTER THIRTY-NINE

SERENA

I shouldn't be here, shouldn't, shouldn't, shouldn't, sitting across from il Dottore with his ugly gaze weighing me in the balance. Surely this one can be broken. Surely this one can be made to bleed.

How could he not remind me of my father?

I beg for release, for annihilation, even for true insanity, the confusion of the damned. I am no longer of use to my family. When I look up, nothing looks back, every dream's dark underbelly now exposed.

Our father had a special closet for his daughter, the doorway overlapped by sheets of cardboard so that no light penetrated, not a ray, the black absolute, the bottom of a coal mine or an ocean. And God help Carolyn Grand if she peeled back that cardboard, God help her if she disobeyed, God help her if she hoped.

I'm in that closet now, though nothing in il Dottore's office has changed: the antiques in the same niches, the amber lamp resting on his desk, the rug cool and gray, the lacquered desk as black as Hank Grand's soul.

Carolyn didn't rebel, no more than the other children who passed through her father's home, accompanied by their own fathers, their own mothers, pledged offerings to some demon too hideous to be named.

Can you commit suicide if you don't exist? Can you kill the self without killing the body?

"Serena, I presume." Il Dottore's tone is almost gay.

"Yes."

"Can you speak a bit louder?"

"No."

"No?"

"No, I can't. Too tired."

"I see. Well, did you at least bring the memos? The ones I asked Kirk to make sure came along with your next visit?"

"I'm sorry, I didn't."

He falls back in his chair, shakes his head and rubs at his eyes, the attempt to feign exasperation supremely theatrical. He persists nevertheless, only gradually calming.

"Alright, let's talk about anger, Serena. Your name, you know, indicates serenity, but is it possible to be serene after what you've been through?"

"Are you asking Serena. Or are you asking Carolyn Grand?"

"Serena."

"Well, the question itself is invalid."

"How so?"

"You assume that anger and serenity are opposed sides of a two-sided coin. So narrow, Doctor, so lacking in imagination, you the scientist, the objectivist. But why not despair?

Why not, when anger is pushed to the side, acknowledge how meaningless, how absurd, how comical your suffering has been? Why not admit that the well you stumbled into has no bottom? May I tell you a story?"

His blue eyes light up. "Of course."

"Other children passed through Hank Grand's house, brought there by a parent or by parents, mother and father, seeming natural, this is what we do, tell no one, it's okay little girl, darling boy. And what are the children to do, broken as they are to the plow? Except, when the adults dismiss them, play?

"For about a year, when Carolyn was seven, Mira, also seven, came to the house at least once a week, not afraid, not even resigned, brought by her father, one of Hank Grand's best buddies and a partner in the film business. First things first, the girls made flesh the perverted fantasies of the adults around them, afterward retreating to Carolyn's bedroom upstairs, to watch TV sometimes but mostly to play a game of pretend. Each of them had a doll, Mira's nearly new, Carolyn's battered, the difference not occurring to the girls as they imagined a world they'd never known. The dolls had parties, went to school, rode three-wheelers up and down the block, played hopscotch on the sidewalk, tested hairstyles, modeled the dresses brought by Mira. They lived happy lives, joyous lives, normal lives, children's lives.

"Other children, when they appeared, were drafted into the game, becoming teachers and doctors and policemen, becoming grocers and druggists, becoming boyfriends and girlfriends, husbands and wives, having children of their own, cherished beloved children.

"Carolyn dreamed, too, and she didn't stop until she was taken away from her father, when her dreams should have come true, when she might have found someone to love her, to cherish her, but got the Acevedas instead. Only then did hope die, replaced by . . . by me, Eleni, Martha, Victoria, Kirk and many, many more. We're her consolation prize."

"Why are you telling me this?"

"I thought you wanted to know."

"Know what exactly? What was your purpose?"

Without warning, I feel myself surrounded, as though wrapped in protective arms, the arms of a lover or a parent. I think, first, it must be Eleni or Kirk, but it's not, and it's not Martha, not Victoria. Older now, older than time itself, Tina holds me.

I listen to us breathe, my breath and hers, feel her warmth, our warmth, the heat of our body. My need swells as though summoned by a snake charmer's flute. It flows into little Tina and I sense obligation, raw as winter rain, when her arms tighten around me.

"You have only to endure," she tells me. "Only to endure."

Il Dottore clears his throat. "You didn't answer my question. The story you told me, about the other children, what did you hope to accomplish?"

"I wanted to inform."

"Please." Il Dottore's laugh is a snort, the grunt of animal, a pig smelling the odor of a truffle beneath the muck at the bottom of its pen. "Inform me of what?"

"That Carolyn never gave up, that her courage, insignificant as it may have been, must count for something, no matter the world schemed against her, no respite, neither water for the thirsty nor food for the starving. Carolyn never caught a break, bad luck her only luck, and still she fought."

"If you only knew how tiresome . . ." He fetches his enameled fountain pen, removes the top, replaces it. "We go round and round. Not just you, Serena, but all of you, Kirk, Victoria, Martha, Eleni, Tina. All of you, without exception. Do any of you have the slightest interest in reintegrating? Into again becoming Carolyn Grand? I don't think so. You want only to be free, of the review board, of your therapy and your therapist."

Does he realize that integration equals annihilation, that we know ourselves as living independent beings, our right to life as valid as that of the first microbe to wriggle its way through a primeval swamp? Just now my bladder is so full it's all I can do not to squirm on the seat. And a little wave of acid inches along my esophagus—the antacid in my bag, so close, relief at hand if only I dared—and there's a dried booger clinging to the inside of my right nostril and my ragged toenails are tearing into my forest-green leggings.

I am real. I exist.

I hear Victoria's voice at that moment, repeat her words, syllable for syllable—careful, careful—there must be no mistakes. "Jesus instructs us to love our enemies, failure to do so a stone rolled across the entrance to His Father's kingdom. But the instruction is no more than a tease because Jesus fails to tell us *how* to love our enemies, as if we could simply decide and our hearts would overfill. You also tease when you, a man able to sustain the illusion of a single self, state our goal simply: reunify. You cannot, of course, understand why the merits of the goal you set are dubious, but that's of no matter. The merits, even if indisputable, are of no value merely stated. You haven't told us how we are to achieve unification any more than Jesus told us how to love those we hate. Wishing, Doctor, let me assure you, will not make it so."

Il Dottore stares at me for a moment, then laughs again. "Let me give you a hint. The path to unification necessarily begins with a commitment to unify. Neither you nor the others have made that commitment." He exudes a theatrical groan and I find myself wondering if he believes what he says. Victoria and Martha would like nothing more than to see me go, accompanied in the shortest of orders by Eleni and Kirk. Martha's said so many times.

"Maybe it's my fault," he continues. "Maybe there's a magic wand out there and I simply haven't found it. It hardly matters because, bottom line, I can't perpetuate a fraud by continuing to treat you when months have gone by and you've made no progress. I really must reconsider our relationship."

CHAPTER FORTY

SERENA

I'm still two blocks from home, hurrying beneath a pewter-gray sky streaked with black clouds that lower by the second, as always oblivious to weather forecasts, each day presumed to repeat the day before. My fellow citizens hustle along beside me, a sprinter in running gear, a mom pushing a stroller, a man who slaps frantically at the tires of his wheelchair. I'm moving a lot faster, too, but not fast enough, a few drops instantly becoming millions upon millions. I know I should see what's there, should reach for a world far older than ours, the great surrender. That's my job, but I'm not up to it. If I ever was.

I have an umbrella in my bag, one of those tiny folding umbrellas barely wide enough to cover my head. I grip the shaft in my right hand, hold down one edge of the fabric with my left, tuck my head between the struts, my clothing instantly soaked, rainwater flowing in streams the length of my body, exquisitely cold. The sidewalks empty as I push through, the cars on the street almost invisible, shrouded in the mist thrown up by their hissing tires.

I'm turning onto South Portland Avenue when I'm attacked fifty yards from home, thinking already of a warm shower and whatever meal can be put together. He's on me before I know he's there, fists slamming into my head, my face, my mouth, my nose. I taste blood on my tongue as I crash to the sidewalk, him on top of me, the weight unbearable as he drags my head back and forth across the concrete, hits me again, again, again while he talks to me, the words little more than grunts.

Confess, innocent, you better, better, better, next time you're dead.

He stands up finally, backing slightly away. I know what he's going to do and I know what Tina meant when she told me that I had only to endure. He lifts his right leg, draws it back, hesitates for seconds that seem like hours, finally drives the tip of his boot into my forehead.

Two women, one of them speaking words I can't hear, slide me onto a hard, plastic board and begin to strap me down. I'm feeling no pain though I'm sure that I will, and soon. The right side of my face is numb, lower back as well, but I'm moving my legs as I offer myself and whoever else may be listening a conclusive self-diagnosis. Carolyn Grand will live.

They lift me up and my world begins to spin, only one more thought before I'm unconscious. The others, the little Carolyn Grands, the selves now gone. Were they exiled, or, worse, annihilated? Or did they simply give up, the struggle subject to the strictest of cost-benefit analyses, too great to be endured?

Hours later, I open one eye, the eye not swollen shut. I'm looking through a window at the blank night sky, my brain numbed by whatever opiate they've put into my system, yet the pain somehow still there, lying outside my body, waiting, waiting. I hear myself groan when I turn my head, the sound remote, my body following in slow motion, sultry almost, as if a lover awaited me, arms outstretched, lips already parted. But there's no lover nearby, only the face of Detective Ortega, his gaze as always intense.

And me, Serena, I'm so relieved to see him that tears well up.

Ortega disappears for a moment, then returns with a Styrofoam cup in his hand, a pink straw poking through its lid. He places the straw between my lips, waits for me to sip, then asks, "Who?"

"Serena."

"Name me a name, Serena. Who attacked you?"

"O'Neill."

Ortega's on his cell phone within seconds, saying, "Yeah, she just identified O'Neill. It's a go." He listens for a moment, then hangs up and returns to my bedside.

"Mirror," I say, but it comes out "miwaw," and I have to repeat myself three times before Ortega understands. I expect him to argue, to beg me to wait until the swelling goes down, until I'm beautiful again, as beautiful as Eleni, but he doesn't. He fetches my purse from a patient's locker, rummages through until he finds a small compact, opens it, places the glass before my single functioning eye. I'm as expected, one side of my swollen face as smooth and round as an overstretched balloon, the skin red turning blue, nose covered with gauze, a line of stitches running across the right side of my forehead. I've seen this face before, courtesy of our dead daddy, though he never let his daughter get within a thousand yards of a hospital, she left to heal on our own. Or not.

"They want to keep you here overnight," Ortega tells me. "Possible concussion. The rest of it"—he shrugs—"the rest of it will heal in time."

He stares at me for a long moment, his eyes flicking between emotions I can't name, then pulls a chair close to the bed, sits down and takes my hand. "It never ends for you, does it?" He leans forward to kiss me, the touch of his lips a passing of feathers across my brow, and I know he loves us. "Rest now, Serena. I'll stay with you as long as I can."

CHAPTER FORTY-ONE

VICTORIA

It's ten o'clock in the morning. We're about to be discharged from Kings County Hospital although our body's in no shape, our mind either after an interview by a psychologist named Lynch, she from the looney ward in another part of the hospital. Did we do this to ourselves? Oh, not literally, but does something in our bizarre affect draw male violence to us? More importantly, is Carolyn Grand's current environment insufficiently protective?

I tell her to call our lawyer, tell her three times before my swollen mouth forms the words precisely enough to be understood. Then she backs off.

Five minutes later a nurse informs me that I'm to be discharged as soon as the paperwork's completed.

"You'll be just fine, dear. No lasting damage."

I hobble to the patient's locker on the other side of the room, no escape from the pain now. My lower back is on fire.

The clothing I discover in a plastic bag, Serena's clothes, are soaking wet, yet I'm to somehow put the garments on my body, bra and panties, skirt and blouse, wet socks, wet shoes. Then I'm to take my fastidious self home via public transportation.

There's a mirror on the inside of the door. My face is the color of an eggplant and hideously swollen, the right side especially. My nose, with the bandages removed, is thick and cut on the side. The upper and lower lids of my right eye are so swollen they meet. Like a pair of lips.

I touch the line of stitches on my forehead, thinking, *Oh, yeah, why leave Frankenstein out.*

"Hey . . ."

I turn to find the cop, Ortega, standing inside the door, a tote bag in his left hand, a set of car keys dangling from the fingers of his right.

"I brought some dry clothes from your apartment."

He steps forward, lays the tote bag on the bed, looks back at me. Only then do I remember that I'm wearing a hospital gown that stops north of midthigh. And nothing else.

"I'll wait outside," he says. "But tell me . . ." He hesitates, his smile apologetic. "Well, who am I talking to? With your face the way it is, you all look alike."

I can't help myself. I return his smile as best I can. "Victoria. Now, get out."

"The first thing I want to know is how you got into the apartment."

It sounds like I'm speaking through a gag, every word muffled, but after a short pause, he answers.

"Serena gave me the key. Last night." He pulls the car into traffic, straightens out. "By the way, I met your neighbor,

Marshal, the one who reeks of marijuana. He knew about the attack because we had the building canvassed for witnesses. Several other buildings, too. Unfortunately, it was raining so hard nobody saw anything. The security cameras were also useless. It doesn't matter now that you've identified—"

"Not me."

It's drizzling and I watch the spots accumulate on the windshield. I have a million questions, but there's no getting the words out, the effort to speak past my injuries too great. Still, that I'm in a car, traveling in private and not on a bus trying to shield my face seems almost miraculous.

"Right, not you. Serena's identification. O'Neill's still on the run, by the way, so you'll have to be careful. Very, very careful. But think about the consequences. O'Neill will be remanded without bail as a parole violator the minute he's taken into custody. You don't get a lawyer when you're on parole, or a trial. You get a hearing, a short one at that, and if the hearing officers don't like what they hear, you're sent back to serve your original sentence. Plus, the new charges don't go away and the years keep piling up."

I wait until Ortega works his way around the back end of a double-parked taxi, then say, "What do they call you?"

It comes out: "Wha day ca ruuuuuu."

Ever the lady, I repeat myself. This time my speech bears a close enough resemblance to the English language to be understood.

"The name on my birth certificate is Roberto. But I'm Bobby to my friends."

"Are you our friend? Are you here in your capacity as a friend?"

He turns from Clarkson Avenue onto Flatbush, staring straight ahead for several blocks until we're again stopped by a light. Then he says, "I read Hank Grand's file. I know what he did to you."

"Fine, so you pity us. But I asked if you're a friend." I have to repeat myself, but not because he doesn't understand. I'm thinking he can't answer the question for himself. In the end, though, he doesn't have a choice.

"If Eleni were only Eleni, the answer would be obvious. But she's not." He looks at me for a moment, eyes fixed on my injuries. "If wanting to help you means I'm your friend, then I'm your friend. Except that I can't help you. I can only watch." Ortega's foot slides to the brake as a cyclist veers into his path. "Okay, let me explain how it works. As detectives, me and Greco gather evidence. We can make an arrest anytime, but unless the suspect is likely to flee, we don't decide on our own. We take our evidence to the squad commander, Lieutenant Ford. She'll either authorize the arrest or ask us to dig up more evidence. But even if she okays the arrest, the issue's not settled. There's a unit in the district attorney's office that liaisons with precinct detectives, especially on major cases. Keep in mind, cops only need probable cause before making an arrest, but prosecutors have to prove guilt beyond a reasonable doubt. So, the DA's office may refuse to arraign a suspect until we produce more evidence. In your case, if you're indicted, your defense will be handled by a special division inside Legal Aid devoted to major prosecutions. That alone makes ADAs cautious. Remember, cops advance their careers by making arrests, prosecutors by securing convictions or guilty pleas."

I don't protest when Ortega—I can't bring myself to call him Bobby, not yet—parks the car and walks me to our apartment. Nor when he runs out to the store and returns with groceries. But I'm feeling—things, sensations, deep dark desires?—maybe for the first time, despite the pain, despite a fear I've carried for all of my life. I know the others, especially Martha, think I'm attracted to women—I thought so myself—but in truth I've been little more than a spayed cat. What other choice did I have? Eleni's promiscuity? Which still threatens us with catastrophic consequences? Better to remain the asexual child Carolyn Grand might have been.

I watch Ortega put the groceries away, watch his eyes as he comes back into the living room. I'm on the couch, lying down, the better side of my face on a throw pillow. Despite the pain, I lurch into a sitting position and motion him over. He looks down at me, his eyes as searching as my own. What, exactly, are we, Bobby and I, looking at? Who's on the other end of the line? I take his hand, and I mumble, "Flank uuuu."

Ortega lays the back of his hand against the side of my face. "I have to get going," he tells me. "We've got two other cases working and I'm the lead on both. Luck of the draw."

The irony doesn't escape me as I watch him head for the door, a testosterone-oozing cop with a heart of gold.

"I want to hear your story," I tell him. "It's only fair."

I have to repeat myself before he gets it. Then he laughs, and his hand rises to his chest as I imagine it rising to Eleni's breast.

"Next time, Victoria, assuming you want to see my ugly face again. Oh, by the way, I asked Marshal to stay with you, at least for tonight. He'll come over about seven. Until then, jam a chair under the knob and keep something, a knife, close to you."

"Do you mean the knife you confiscated?"

I'm expecting a laugh, but Ortega bites at his lower lip, then squats. He lifts the cuff on his right pant leg and withdraws a small revolver from a holster fastened to his ankle. He lays the revolver on top of the memos on our table.

"O'Neill's breaking down," he explains. "He's spent most of his life in a cage for extremely violent crimes and now he knows he's going back. Somebody has to pay, Victoria. And that somebody, right now, is you."

"And I'm supposed to just shoot him?"

"Actually, you do have an alternative. You can give O'Neill what he wants. You can confess to killing your father. Not a strategy I'd recommend, by the way. But neither is letting O'Neill beat you to death. Don't underestimate the threat." He pauses, waiting, perhaps, for me to laugh. When I don't, he continues, his tone now sober. "What I think is that Detective Greco, if he can't put the murder on someone else, is gonna take a shot at you. He's gonna put you in a little room, apply pressure and see what pops out. It's not that he thinks you're guilty. It's that you might be and he has nothing to lose."

CHAPTER FORTY-TWO
MARTHA

Zenia,

How many times have you warned me against unrestrained arrogance? How many times urged me to resist embracing my bottom-line narcissism? How many times have you pressed me to accept the occasional defeat? If not with good grace, at least with resignation.

What, you've run out of fingers and toes? You're now working with grains of sand?

I can't beat them. I admit that to you, put it in writing, cannot take it back. The collection of identities calling itself Carolyn Grand will not be manipulated by Dr. Laurence Halberstam. The only confession in the offing is my own. I've failed.

Between Carolyn's many years in therapy and her sharp, neatly-concealed intelligence, her identities have become emotionally self-sufficient. One imagines them a family on the frontier, mountain people who keep to themselves, who reflexively fear the outsider.

Given the lives they've been forced to live, one can hardly blame them.

But I will never reach them. They parry each thrust with some tidbit, an anecdote, a memory, real, imagined, or entirely fictional. And the identity you wish to speak with is never there.

I didn't exist. I didn't exist. I didn't exist.

Admit defeat, face your failures, cut your losses. That's always been your advice—it's why you settled the lawsuit—and I'm ready to take it. In any event, I'll be telling no lie when I inform the review board that Carolyn Grand's therapy has gone nowhere, that I hold no hope for the future and that I must, therefore, conclude our professional relationship.

What then?

That's up to the board, of course. They may choose to leave Carolyn Grand at home until they locate another therapist. Or they may choose to confine her. Confining her is the safest course and the one they wish to take, but Carolyn's attorney is unusually zealous, so . . .

You asked about Patricia, my little chubby, the idiot I told to lose a hundred pounds if she wished to free herself from the delusions that torment her existence. My apologies, Zenia, I've been so obsessed with my little multi that I've lost perspective. In any event, Patricia accepted the challenge. She's dropped fifty pounds and taken to wearing tiny thongs that cause her buttocks to literally undulate. I need only snap my fingers and . . . and I believe I will.

I'm going to leave it there for the time being. I'm dining with Marilyn and Bill this evening and I need to prepare myself. My sister is beyond tedious and her husband is even worse. So sincere, so mediocre, so ultimately boring.

Zenia, I'll be thinking of you as I shovel Marilyn's breaded pork chops into my mouth, comparing your conversation with hers, all those forbidden rooms through which only the great may pass. Perhaps that will see me through. Let us hope so.

Always yours, Laurence

We gathered within seconds, all except Tina. Though we read the email over and over, the message never eluded us. Despite the bullshit, Halberstam wasn't resigned to his failure. The scumbag was out for revenge.

What to do about it? How much risk were we prepared to accept? The cop was there, Ortega. Eleni's madly in love with him, though she won't admit it. Talk about risk. I like the cop. We all do. But trust him? Give me a fucking break. For all I know, the freak named Carolyn Grand might amount to no more than a notch on Ortega's belt. Eleni is blind to the threat, and there's not one of us who wants to bring her back to Earth. She's positively glowing, as if she's shed a decade. If anything, we're jealous.

At his insistence, the cop's driving me to Halberstam's office. O'Neill's still out there he claims, growing more desperate and more dangerous by the day. So, we definitely need protection. I like to think I can take care of myself, but after checking my face in the mirror, my resistance fades.

"You want me to go up with you?" he asks. We're parked twenty yards from Halberstam's door.

"To do what? Shoot him?"

He only smiles as he turns on the radio. "Good luck, Martha."

I take my seat, Halberstam's office now so familiar I might as well be standing on a subway platform. I'm holding a manila envelope in my lap and the doctor's eyes go to it after a quick survey of our injuries. Injuries in which, apparently, he has no interest.

"Ah, the memos at last."

"'Fraid not, Doctor."

Halberstam's chin jerks up. Whatever's about to come, it won't be good. My tone is too cold even to be confrontational. No more dancing around the ring. Toe-to-toe.

"I have something you need to see," I explain. "But I'm going to tell you a story first. Just so you fully understand our position. Not my position, Doctor. Our position."

"Is that so?" Halberstam's eyes withdraw. If he's angry, he's not showing it. "I have news for you as well. But we'll save that for later on. Proceed."

"You age out of foster care on your eighteenth birthday. So long, goodbye, adios. You know nothing of the real world, even if you're sane. But if your fragmented psyche grows more fragmented every day, you are well and truly fucked. Carolyn Grand was first sent to a shelter where she was raped on her second day. She then took to the streets, sleeping in the subway or on a park bench when it was warm enough. Chaos swirled around her. No, I should say that chaos swirled around *them* because there were so many little Carolyns that it was all-but-impossible to keep track.

"Carolyn's memory became a series of discrete patches separated by empty black holes. Fall asleep in Manhattan, wake up in Brooklyn. And that guy you traded sex for shelter with because you couldn't bear another cold night on the street? He's a complete stranger to the Carolyn who wakes up the next morning. What's more, he's demanding sex and he's not taking no for an answer. A deal is, after all, a deal.

"Survival at its most basic level demands knowledge that can pass from one self to another. Where to get a free meal. A talent for begging. Instinctive avoidance of dangerous people and places. Where you can find a clean bathroom to empty your bowels.

"You're assaulted from time to time. There's no avoiding it on the street, but you learn to minimize the damage. From time to time, one or another of the city's social workers finds you shelter in a protected environment. But then you disappear for a month. Or forget the arrangement was ever made."

I stop long enough to smile. "I keep saying 'you' as if there were only one of us, when in fact we were closer to a tribe. We remained that way throughout our stay at Creedmoor and afterward, until our involuntary commitment to Brooklyn Psychiatric, where we lived for almost a year.

"We were a source of conflict on the medical side at Brooklyn Psychiatric. Psychologists urged group and individual therapy. Psychiatrists preferred obliteration through chemicals. Neither treatment was of any value, but still we benefited. We benefited by eating three reasonably nutritious meals each day, by sleeping each night in the same bed, by having our medical needs met. Including an ulcer on our right leg that had been open for a month.

"By the time we encountered a hospital social worker named Evelyn Scaparelli, we were physically stable. We were also secure enough in our day-to-day survival to understand, despite the antipsychotic meds, the opportunity she presented. We were entitled by law, she explained, to benefits like disability, Medicaid, SNAP, and Section Eight. Put them all together, and it amounted to a stable life, a springboard if you will, a platform. But only if we became responsible enough to maintain it. Each of these benefits requires reauthorization, at which time documents have to be produced. Your latest bank statement, latest disability statement, SNAP benefit statement, a notarized application. For the average American, the process would be merely annoying. For Carolyn Grand and her merry band . . .

"Victoria and I were born while Carolyn was in Brooklyn Psychiatric. Victoria won't admit it, but I believe that what was left of Carolyn Grand deliberately created us. That's how much it meant to come home at night, to lock the door behind you and know you were safe. The other selves, they could enjoy their shelter, but they could never have maintained it. Me and Victoria, we did that. Against crazy odds at first but always stubbornly, obsessively. Always focused on a single goal. A locked door between us and the world, a door you could open and close, people you could let in or leave out. Keep in mind, Doctor, these were luxuries that Carolyn had never known."

Halberstam finally intervenes. "Why," he asks, "are you telling me this? Why now?"

"Because we want you to understand what the stakes are. For us, I mean. What it means to us when we read something like this."

I slip the top sheet from the manila envelope, work my way out of the submissive seat, walk over to his desk and lay the email we intercepted last night in his hand. He glances down, a sneer on his face, then blanches, his complexion turning bone white.

"What do you think might happen," I ask him, "if we stake out your office until Patricia shows up? What might happen if we give her this email?" I reach into the envelope and withdraw a second email, this the earliest, where he tells Zenia that Patricia has a rich daddy who molested her.

"What do you think would happen if I run down Patricia's father and show him the email labeling him a pedophile? How long before he files a malpractice suit? Hours? Minutes? Seconds?" I hesitate, a practiced comedian about to deliver a punch line. "You're licensed by New York's Department of Health. Imagine standing before one of their review boards, explaining why you passed on confidential information about a patient to your fucking guru. Or how you intend to seduce Patricia now that she's lost enough weight to be attractive. Your license, your accreditations . . . out the window, Doctor. And we both know it."

Halberstam's blues eyes close, but not before I register the panic. I watch him draw a long breath as he gathers what little courage he possesses. He's going to bluff and I'm going to call. A long stay at a psychiatric hospital means the loss of our apartment. We'd have to start over and I haven't the heart for the struggle.

"You stole these somehow," he says, his tone unsteady. "You invaded my privacy. I could send you to prison."

"You're right about the stealing, Doctor, and about us invading your privacy. And you're also right about that invasion being a crime. But on the last part you're not even close. Carolyn Grand's a certified lunatic and they don't send lunatics to prison. They send them to the looney bin, which is exactly where you want to send her anyway. Talk about lose-lose. This is lose-lose-lose, the last loser being you." I slap the top of the desk. Something's happening to us, even beyond the many threats. We've been cringing all our lives and we're sick of it. We no longer hope to survive. We mean to survive. "You spelled out what we want in your emails. We want to be rid of you, of you and of all supervision. Simple as that."

I drop three more emails on his desk, then walk back to my chair and sit down. Last night, Bobby insisted that Halberstam's life was entirely transactional. A series of deals from which he hoped to profit. If he found he couldn't, he'd cut his losses and walk away. The cop was right, and I can read it in Halberstam's eyes when he raises his head. He's going to make the only move on the table.

"You'll have to admit, my evaluation of Carolyn Grand and her identities was dead on. You're more than a match. In fact, you remind me of Zenia." Having delivered the ultimate compliment, he steeples his fingers. "So, how shall we proceed?"

CHAPTER FORTY-THREE

ELENI

We're in a rowboat on the lake in Prospect Park. Bobby and me, with the rest of the gang, excepting Tina, hovering about. This is something new, the lack of privacy, the pack animal mentality. I don't like it, but I can't do anything about the situation. I couldn't prevent Serena's and Bobby's inevitable coupling either. With Victoria next in line. We're like infatuated teenagers, nobody stopping to ask what's in it for Bobby. And I'm not coming from the same place as Kirk and Martha. I don't think Bobby's setting us up. No, I think he's as crazy as we are. I don't know why because I'm afraid to ask. I'm afraid to break the spell, to lose the lover I only just found.

Why else would he put up with the chaos? If he weren't crazy? Why would he accommodate himself to whoever showed up? At one point, Martha went into the kitchen to prepare dinner and Kirk returned. That left Bobby to cook the meal, which he cheerfully did. After dinner, he and Kirk watched a Yankees baseball game, both of them big-time fans.

Bobby slept on the couch that night when I know he was hoping I'd arrive any minute. I wanted to, clad in a see-through body stocking, but I couldn't.

We're well into October now, with no sign of Alfred O'Neill. The consensus is that he's fled the city. The weather is fine, the sky blue, the sun bright enough to dazzle, the leaves on the trees at the water's edge still dark and green. I'm watching a family of geese a couple of hundred yards away while Bobby rows, his strokes languid enough to arouse. He approaches sex in much the same way, taking his time, reading my cues, all in that laid-back cop style. He claims my body talks to him. If so, I know what it's saying: Oh god, oh god, oh god, oh god.

"It's going to get rough now." He sighs as he raises the oars, allowing the boat to drift. "Our squad commander, Lieutenant Ford, she's feelin' a lot of heat. That's because police departments across the country live and die by their homicide clearance rates. And maybe some cases can't be closed, but this one, according to the bosses at the Puzzle Palace, should have been a slam dunk."

"Let me guess, Ford's transferring that heat to Detective Greco."

"Right, plus Homicide's an elite unit. You earn your way up to Homicide and you can earn your way back down. Greco's sweating, but he doesn't have enough to make an arrest. Of you, O'Neill, or any of the other suspects."

"What about the DNA?"

"Still out. But I uncovered another hooker down at the hotel who maybe saw you. She's not sure, couldn't swear in court, but it was probably you. That's two now."

The words sting: *I uncovered*. I want to ask him how hard he worked to find her, how many hours stalking the halls of the Golden Inn. A waste of time because I know the answer. He'll do his job and let the cards fall where they may. I have to wonder what advice he offers Greco.

"There's some good news," he continues. "We reviewed the footage from the security cameras near the entrance to your building. You didn't come through that door, going in either direction, on the night your father was killed."

"You already told us that."

"I know, but that's not the good news. You could have gone down the fire escape and through the alley to South Oxford Street without being seen. It wouldn't be easy, but it's still possible. Greco's trying to sell that theory to the lieutenant, but she's not buying. And if he can't sell it to Ford, no prosecutor is likely to sell it to a jury. That's the good news."

I let it go at that, my father's death now seeming as remote as his life when he was safely behind bars. I watch Bobby drop the oars into the water, listen to the slap of the small waves against the side of the boat. There's enough breeze to work its way through my hair. It teases my scalp as I've been teasing Bobby ever since we left the house. A quick touch, a laying of my hand on his shoulder, a smile that fades, slowly, into a promise. I lean forward now to caress the side of his face, but I'm interrupted by a tremendous squawking.

Behind me, the geese leap up, wings beating frantically as they lift their bodies clear of the water. They run then, webbed feet slapping the surface until they finally rise, still calling to each other. Bobby waits until the din recedes, then tells me, "I won't be around for a while. I've been ordered to keep away from you. By Lieutenant Ford, so it counts."

"Does that mean someone ordered you to approach us in the first place?"

"No, that was my own idea." He brings the oars onto the boat and reaches for me. "What a woman you are," he whispers. "I'm crazy for you." Then I'm in his arms, our mouths locked together, my hands gathered at the back of his head, pulling him closer. But he lets me go just as suddenly as he reached out for me, his look darkening.

"Make sure everyone understands, Eleni. First thing, if you see Greco's face in the doorway, ask for a lawyer. Don't wait."

"And that will bring everything to a stop?"

"Probably not, but get it on the record, especially if there's a neighbor close enough to hear."

CHAPTER FORTY-FOUR

SERENA

He comes for me two days later at ten o'clock in the night, Detective Greco by himself. I'm looking out the window when he pulls up, watching a steady rain spatter across the sidewalk and the street. Greco's driving a black car, perfectly anonymous, backing it into a narrow parking space, stepping out, hustling through the rain, all business, the postman on his rounds. He rings our bell, the intercom, my first instinct to hide behind the couch, under the bed, in the closet, anywhere Daddy can't find me. Because I'm all alone, my sisters and brother far distant, as though I'd made them up, imagined or dreamed them, our years together an extravagant hallucination.

I press the buzzer, let Greco inside, stand by the door waiting for him to walk up the stairs. Our elevator stands idle on the first floor, three days awaiting a repairman who never comes, I hear Greco's footfalls, heavy, plodding, steady, determined. He's coming for me, I'm trapped, I search for my family again, but there's no one, no one, no one.

Then the door opens, and I'm looking into Greco's tiny green eyes. He appears tired, shoulders slumped, a day's stubble making its way along his jowls to the collar of his shirt. "A few things we gotta clear up," he tells me. "Down at the precinct."

"I don't want to speak to you without a lawyer present."

I'm proud of myself. I remembered. But Greco's ready for me. He shakes his head and says, "You're not a suspect, Ms. Grand. You're a person of interest. Lawyers are only for suspects."

Bobby warned us, but I'm still not ready, never will be, a coward to my bones and why am I put here to wage a battle I've always lost, never won? Why not Kirk or Eleni or Martha? I have no fight in me.

"I'd like to call a lawyer before we go, detective."

"You'll have plenty of time to do that at the station." He glances at his watch. "This shouldn't take long, so why don't you just make it easy. If not, I'm gonna have to put you in handcuffs."

His voice tightens, as if he's become angry, as if he'd like nothing more than to humiliate me—no point to saying *us* because there's no us listening—and he's hoping I'll resist. I resist anyway, feebly, true, but still I do resist.

"Am I under arrest?"

"You're not even a suspect. You're a person of interest."

"But I can't call a lawyer?"

He slides his hand beneath his jacket to a pair of handcuffs dangling from a belt loop. "Look, it's not my intention to get nasty, but there's a few things we have to resolve at the precinct and I'm parked by a hydrant. So, you pick, Ms. Grand. Cuffs or compliance."

* * *

The descent is deliberate, through the doors of the Eighty-Fourth Precinct, looking like a small school from the outside but suddenly a cop world, the wicked brought to justice, the virtuous irrelevant, go find yourself a guru, evil abides here and there's only us cops to keep it contained. Cops swirl about us, cops and suspects, three women chained to a bench, a man in a corner who smells of urine and feces and death. I'm led through the lobby up the stairs to a deserted room, eight metal desks arranged in back-to-back pairs, a room to the side, glass fronted, three closed doors in the back, windows to the side of each. The light is dim and objects seems to float, but then Greco flicks the light switches to his left and my new world reveals itself: dreary, workaday, without inspiration. He leads me between the desks to the middle door in the back. No explanation given, he opens the door to a tiny room, a window that's a mirror from inside, three chairs and a tiny desk, graffiti-covered cinderblock walls. I sit in the chair facing the window-mirror without being asked.

"I just gotta set a few things up, then I'll be back." Greco lifts my purse from my lap. "Now, I didn't search you for a weapon, which I really should of done, but I'm gonna have to look through your purse. Meanwhile, you try to relax. If you need anything, there'll be someone outside."

Then he's out the door, taking my purse and the cell phone we might (but don't) have with him. I know it's deliberate, a kidnapping really, an abduction, but it's not my body he wants or my money. It's my liberty, our liberty. Someone has to pay and beggars like Greco can't be choosers. There are no cameras in this room, no witnesses, my word against his if he claims I never asked for a lawyer.

Time consumes my spirit, I've no watch to count the seconds, the minutes, the hours, but each unit gnaws at me. I know I'm supposed to draw on some kernel of resolve, to gird my loins for the battle sure to come. But I'm helpless, only wishing for oblivion as I've been wishing all along. I'm not up to this, not sufficiently courageous or stubborn or defiant, never was and never hope to be, my purpose in the greater scheme of Carolyn Grand residing on the opposite end of any spectrum you'd care to name. And who's to help me now?

I read the graffiti on the walls, as I imagine every suspect confined alone to this small space has, a step forward, a step to the side, the walls too ugly to touch. FREEDOM FOR ALL; RESIST; NEVER PICK UP A DEAD MAN'S GUN; WE ONLY HAVE TO BE LUCKY ONCE; KILL ALL COPS. I'm wondering how they did it—in here, close confined—and if they were punished when the detectives returned. Were they slapped, punched, did they scream out their defiance as they wiped the blood from their many faces?

And where is Bobby right now, right this minute?

I know my every move has been choreographed: you will pace, you will read the graffiti, you will curse yourself and your fate, you will, finally, try the door that you know is unlocked, just to see if maybe Greco was bluffing, maybe there's no one out there. But there is, of course, a police woman who barely looks up before I'm back inside, the door closed, trapped and afraid.

The door reopens only a minute later, the same policewoman, short, stocky, a block of flesh, eyes as cold as they are indifferent. She wears a wedding ring on a thin gold chain, a widow with mouths to feed.

"I need you to come with me."

"I want to call a lawyer."

"I don't know anything about that. You'll have to speak with the detective. But right now, I need you to come with me."

I realize that's how they do it, dumb insistence, rote repetition, a physical threat at the ready, do it or else. "Where am I going?"

"A lineup."

I'm in a room with five other women, their chatter relaxed. They know each other, cops probably, volunteering in casual dress. I'm in jeans and a red sweater, an outcast nonetheless, standing alone, no one to counsel me. I have to fight for myself. The white paint on the back wall is broken by numbers, one through six, spaced four or five feet apart, ten feet up.

A uniformed cop, an officer, a man, walks into the room, the others hopping to attention, me off alone in a corner. "Almost ready, so let's get under the numbers. And you"—he points to me—"here, number four."

Almost in the middle, I walk up, summoning the will to demand a lawyer, but he holds me off, his tone when he speaks a blank nothing, the voice of a robot. "When your number's called, take three steps forward and wait for further instructions. Don't do anything on your own."

He's retreats and I'm left staring at a mirror I know is a window on the far side, others gathered to bear witness. I want to appeal to the women around me, state my claim of innocence, but I don't really exist for them, just a chore, like morning coffee spilled on the bedroom carpet, blot it up and move on.

The lights brighten and a voice barks through a speaker: "Number one, step forward. Turn to the left. Step back."

I'm taken through the same routine when my turn comes, step forward, turn to the left, step back. The procedure only changes with number six. She's asked to turn to the left, take another step forward, tilt her head down, then it's over and I'm being led back through the building, room by room, the precinct oddly empty this late on a weekday. I follow, tired, disheartened, meek, when the policewoman finally breaks the silence.

"You need to use a bathroom?"

"No, not now."

"Do yourself a favor, lady. Use the bathroom. Who knows how long it'll be until you get another chance."

Her indifferent tone doesn't change, nor does her manner or the reserved distance in her brown eyes. There's just this much, a confession of her own impotence, do the job, do the job, this is all I can give you.

I use the bathroom, splash water on my face and neck, straighten my hair, dry myself with paper towels. I'm turning to go when I feel Tina surround me and I know she's been there all the time. But it's Eleni's voice I hear: "Endure," she tells me. "Endure."

CHAPTER FORTY-FIVE

SERENA

Greco reappears only a minute after the door closes behind me, expression grave, an oncologist delivering bad news. I'm sorry but . . . He shuts the door, drops a stack of files onto the desktop, and sits.

"It ain't good the way it went." He shakes his head. "Two witnesses from the Golden Inn? You remember, right, the Golden Inn where your father was killed? Well, they ID'd you right away. So, I know you were there."

"I wasn't." The words please me in some way, the truth a mere technicality here, but the truth nonetheless.

"Two people saw you there, Carolyn. They're not both wrong."

"I don't make that claim, only that I wasn't there."

Greco lays his hands flat on the desk. He leans forward, mimics my supplicant's tone: "Somebody else was there, another me, but it wasn't me. Okay, I'm willing to play that game. So, let's pretend for a minute. Two witnesses claim they saw Carolyn Grand at the inn, one of them on the stairs, one on the third floor where your old man was killed. That puts Carolyn Grand in the building, at least physically. True?"

If only Eleni were here, or Martha or Kirk, they'd say exactly what I'm thinking: how do I know you aren't lying about the witnesses? Only I can't bring myself to pronounce the words. They won't cross my vocal chords, the barrier physical.

"There is no Carolyn Grand," I finally mutter. "We're a collective."

"I'm not arguing the point. This is more like a hypothetical. If two witnesses ID a suspect within fifty feet of where a man was murdered, and this suspect knew the victim and had a definite grudge against him, what would you think?"

"I wouldn't."

"Wouldn't what?"

"Think."

"If that's the way you want it." He reaches into his jacket pocket, removes a card. "I'm gonna read your rights to you, in case you don't already know 'em. You have the right to remain silent. Anything you say can and will be used against you in a court of law. You have the right to speak to an attorney. If you cannot afford an attorney, one will be provided for you." He slides the card across the desk, along with a pen. "Sign on the bottom, where it says I explained your rights and you understand them."

"If I do, will you get me a lawyer?"

"Absolutely." He watches me sign, then takes back the card and slips it into his pocket. "So, I won't ask any more questions. I'm just gonna talk. But if you should feel the urge to jump in at some point, don't hesitate."

"What about my lawyer?"

"All in good time. Remember, we're just talking here.." Greco rises, removes his jacket, lays it over the back of the chair and sits down, a gun beneath his armpit fully exposed, the maneuver leaving him diminished, no matter his intentions. "Lemme start with this. You had every right to hate your father. Even more, from where I sit, you had the right to kill him. The man who enslaved you as a child was literally stalking you. And he wasn't taking no for an answer. If you disagree with that, say so."

I don't disagree and I don't speak. I'm thinking that my father's death would be a kind of self-defense, except that I can't bring myself to believe that we're capable of murder, the taking of life and light. I don't want to believe it.

"Okay, so that's settled. You have a right to self-defense. Nobody says otherwise. Plus, you reported the stalking to uthorities more than once, but no action was taken. So, I'm sking: What were you supposed to do? Wait around till he aught you alone one day? Were you supposed to hope you urvived, hope you had a chance to report him?"

I can't help it. I raise my hand to my face. The stitches re out and the swelling's mostly gone, the fading bruises ow light enough to conceal with makeup. Yet, despite its erocity, O'Neill's attack was nothing compared to what our ather did to us, did in cold blood, laid-back, enjoying every econd, prolonging the thrill.

"I'm sayin', Carolyn, if I was your lawyer, that's how I'd dvise you to play it. Tell the jury that you went to the Golden nn hoping to convince him to stay away from you. But then e attacked you, maybe tore at your clothes, and you knew that you'd always be in danger as long as Hank Grand drew breath. Crazy with fear and knowing a system that hadn't protected Carolyn Grand in the past couldn't protect her in the future, you exercised the only available option."

Unable to contain myself, I finally speak, as Greco knew I eventually would. I do no more than repeat myself: "I wasn't there." But I know as I say the words that I'll speak again. My world tightens around me. This is unbearable.

"Great, let's say you don't remember." He leans over the desk, taps my forehead, the touch like a hammer blow. "But there's only one brain, Carolyn, which you all share. The memories are stored in that brain, if only you'd take a closer look. So, what I'm gonna do is arrange for that lawyer you mentioned. See, I haven't forgotten. And you, in the meantime, need to think seriously about what I said. The longer you try to evade responsibility, the worse it's gonna look to a jury. And by the way, something I didn't mention. The DNA evidence came back this morning, which is why I picked you up. The witnesses are just icing on the cake."

And so I sit, the seconds piling up, absorbing the final blow, staring at Greco's jacket still hung over the back of his chair. What I'm feeling is desolation, that it should come to this, because if one of us was in that room it could only have been to kill Hank Grand, reconciliation never in the cards for any of us, including our father. I rise and pace the room, three steps forward, three steps back. I can't escape a rising despair, that we're trapped, that our fate was sealed long ago, an accident of birth, that I might as well confess.

Hank Grand lived in a two-story home with a basement and an attic. So many places to hide, it took Daddy forever to find his daughter because she never gave in to his threats, never made a sound. Did she know, absolutely, that he would eventually find her? Or did she, each time, hope to escape him forever? Or was she merely stubborn, fighting back, the beatings inevitable, even (and maybe especially) when she was good?

I feel as though I'm hiding right now, that we've been hiding all our lives, every hideout also a trap. I'm trapped in this room, my world closed off. I stare at the mirror-window, certain I'm being observed, a white rat on the vivisectionist's table. Let's take a look at that liver, that kidney, that heart. Let's core the girl out, leave her empty and lost.

When I can't stand the tension, my nerves screaming, I go to the door and pull it open. My policewoman is in place. She barely looks up. Behind her, Greco's face-to-face with a taller black woman, pleading. The woman's gold badge is pinned to the lapel of a navy suit and she's listening with her arms crossed below her breasts. As I back into my little room, her attention flicks to me for a moment and I'm again that specimen under the microscope, awaiting the touch of a scalpel.

Greco comes in a few minutes later and I'm already thinking you'll never get out of this room unless you give him what he wants. He's all smiles, though, and he's carrying a bag of corn chips and an orange soda.

"I called for that lawyer," he says. "But he might be a while getting here. Bein' as it's so late."

I can't help myself. I open the soda and drink from the bottle, my dry throat responding gratefully to the carbonation, the sugar rush instantaneous.

Greco pulls his chair closer to the small desk between us. "Right, so what we spoke about before, the witnesses, the DNA, you gotta agree with one thing. Carolyn Grand was in that room. If I'm wrong, say so."

I shake my head but decide not to speak.

"Then we agree. Excellent. You were in the hotel on the night your father died, spotted on the third floor where your father rented a room. So, what do you think Carolyn Grand was there to do? Because here's another thing you should know. Hank Grand was unconscious when he was killed." Greco nods his head several times, the gesture seeming rote. "Yeah, that's right. When Carolyn Grand entered her father's room, she found him helpless. Plus, Carolyn knew exactly where her father would be at eight o'clock that night. My partner saw the note."

"I don't have anything to tell you," I explain. "That night is empty, blank, unseen, the far side of a moon I'll never visit because the only way to get there is to die."

"Here we go again. This Carolyn didn't kill her father. A different Carolyn did it. But you will admit that *some* Carolyn drove a knife into Hank Grand's back. Am I right or wrong?"

Greco's asking a direct question and I know I'll never see that lawyer. I look around the room, no tape recorder, no cameras. Greco can do whatever he wants to me, just like Daddy. I start to rise, then slump down again. "I can't speak for anyone else." I'm barely whispering. "I'm not responsible."

"But you do live in the same apartment with all the other, the other whatevers. That's true, right?"

"Yes, it's true."

"And you've been living there for a long time?"

"Yes, right."

"So, if something you use all the time, say every fucking day, suddenly went missing, you'd have to know about it." Greco's smile is wolfish. He's been setting this up from the beginning. "Any knives missing, Carolyn? Any long sharp knives that were there one day and gone the next?"

"I wouldn't know, detective. I don't cook."

"Bullshit." He slaps his palm on the table. "Fuck it. Just fuck it. Everyone says you're crazy, but I'm not buyin'. I think you know exactly what happened and I want you to tell me. So, let's start at the beginning. Your old man hands you a note. The Golden Inn Hotel at eight p.m. You didn't have to go, but you did. Because you were afraid of your father? That makes exactly zero sense. No, you went because you wanted the scumbag out of your life once and for all."

"It's not true."

"Really? You know that for a fact, Carolyn? Because a minute ago you told me you weren't there. You told me you didn't even exist on the night your father was killed. So how can you be sure I'm not right? Unless you've been lying all along." He grinds to a halt, then leans over the desk and sneers. "Time to cut the bullshit, honey. Those movies your father made? The movies with you in 'em? I watched them. We all did, the whole precinct. And there's one I remember especially. You went into the woods to pick berries and stumbled on these boys? Carolyn, I ran that movie four times and one thing I can say for sure. It looked to me like you were enjoying yourself."

The game continues on, Greco alternately berating me and leaving me to stew in the swamp of my own thoughts. I want to give up, to feed Greco whatever he needs to hear even knowing that I can't be held forever. I believe myself eternally damned, a trapped and battered woman seeking any escape, a crack in the wall, a crack in the world, let me out, let me out. Eleni's whispered advice—endure, just endure—becomes my shield, a barrier, not against Greco's assault but against my own words, until Greco's frustration dissolves into sentences that are no more than profanities dangling from a string, until finally the door opens and the black woman I saw earlier appears in the opening.

"Detective, a word outside."

"Lieutenant, please."

"Outside, detective."

I wait and I wait and I wait. I eat the corn chips and I wait. I drink the soda and I wait. I'm expecting an arrest, the physical evidence too strong to ignore. Instead, the door finally opens, and Bobby walks into the room. I should be angry, should be enraged. Instead I'm ready to fall into his arms, to be cradled, to feel my head against his chest. He looks at me for a minute, his features tight, his breath shallow. Finally, he drops his chin and sighs.

"C'mon, Serena, let's go. It's over."

CHAPTER FORTY-SIX

ELENI

We're in Bobby's car and driving before I notice the blood. Bobby's wearing a light-blue shirt and a gray jacket. Both are spattered with tiny red drops. The left side of his face, too, and his hair.

"I didn't rescue Serena," he tells me. "She saved herself, at least temporarily. It was Lieutenant Ford who called a halt. She watched most of the interrogation and she doesn't think Carolyn Grand killed her father. That's because Serena stood up to everything Greco threw at—"

I reach out to stroke the side of his face. "Tell me what happened. No bullshit, Bobby. I'm so tired I'm ready to collapse."

The sun's not quite up yet, but the doughnut shops, the fast-food joints and the diners are doing business. Men and women on their way to work drift through the dawn light. They move toward a subway platform two blocks away. Bobby seems focused on their progress, his eyes moving from side to side. Finally, he speaks.

"O'Neill's dead. I killed him." He flinches and his fingers tighten on the wheel. "I can't really focus on this right now. In fact, I'm supposed to be in an emergency room undergoing some kind of evaluation. But I'm gonna tell you what happened anyway. Just one time, right?"

"Yeah, okay."

"I've been tracking O'Neill ever since he disappeared. I talked to anybody who knew him, sisters, brother, mother, cousins, parolees at the shelter, hookers and pimps at the inn. They wouldn't tell me where he was, if they knew, but they claimed he told people that he wasn't going back to prison. Me, I've done this hundreds of times and I stayed with it until his sister gave him up. According to her, O'Neill borrowed money from the family, then threatened his mother when she asked him to pay it back."

Bobby stops talking, the transition too abrupt, and my first impulse is to fill the empty space. I wait instead, only reaching out to lay my hand on his arm.

"I drove from the sister's apartment in East Harlem," he finally resumes, "to the address she gave me in the Bronx. No way did I intend to knock on the door, so I set up down the block and settled in. He came out an hour later and I confronted him. As it turned out, he meant what he told his sister. He pulled an automatic and got off two shots. They missed." He runs his fingers through his hair but doesn't look at me. "Security cams recorded the confrontation. The shooting was righteous, a hundred percent righteous."

Bobby's tone doesn't project defiance or even certainty. He seems oddly wistful. Far away for now but knowing he'll pay later on. For me, when I finally lock the door to our apartment, I become dizzy with relief. A big part of me thought I'd never see home again.

Bobby reaches out to steady me. "Take it slow, honey. You push it, you'll collapse." He leads me to the couch, sits me down, drops down beside me. I don't have all that many words in me, but I can't contain myself.

"I was only there for bits and pieces of Serena's questioning," I say. "But I have to believe that the only reason Greco didn't arrest us was because he was lying. About the witnesses and the DNA both."

"Exactly right. From what I was told, the two witnesses were so wrecked they had problems standing up. Neither ID'd you in the lineup. As for the DNA, the test results aren't in yet. That's the last barrier, Eleni. You come up clean, you're home free."

We sit for a few minutes, the part about the DNA bouncing through my brain. Then Bobby gets up and walks into the kitchen. He returns with an open bottle of wine and two glasses. I take the glasses from him, watch him fill them halfway, finally hand one back. I drink, drink again, oblivion sounding like a good idea. Sex and booze, a refuge I've embraced many times in the past. But Martha has other ideas.

Ask him, she demands.

I don't want to ask him, now or later. I'm too afraid of the answer, too afraid of losing him, not a cheap fuck in a motel room, but a lover at last.

"Ask him."

This time the voice belongs, not to Martha or Kirk, but to Tina. Tina speaks gently, even regretfully, but there's no escape. I have to ask.

CHAPTER FORTY-SEVEN

ELENI

I put my arm around Bobby's waist and draw him in. My lips find the side of his neck so that when I speak, my mouth is within inches of his ear. "You're a good guy, Bobby."

"You mean the issue was in doubt?"

"Yeah, it was. But there's no issue now. It's not just that you helped us. Others, not many but a few, have done the same. What you've done, my darling, is make yourself part of the family. Well, it's time you told us why. Why would a normal guy involve himself with a psycho named Carolyn Grand? Or five psychos named Carolyn Grand? Or any psychos at all? What's in it for Bobby Ortega?"

He leans over to kiss me and I'm instantly thinking, *Okay, fuck this, let's mess up Martha's bed*. Then he lets me go and sits up straight.

"I stopped needing reasons a while ago," he tells me. "Is that good enough?"

"No, I . . . The thing, Bobby, is that I'm pretty sure that I'm in love with you. But if my sisters and my brother told me to give you up, I would. We've never let anyone into our lives, and maybe it's too late to get started. We have to know."

He slides forward onto the couch. Lays his head on the backrest. "The best I can do is describe the road I walked to get here. Then it's up to you." He slides his arms around my shoulders and pulls me tight against him. "But I just want to ask, before I testify voluntarily, if this is a trial by jury. And if it is, does the verdict have to be unanimous? Can I appeal? Is there a Supreme Court?"

"Uh-uh, Bobby, just a scared little girl who can't afford to lose her way."

"Okay, no more bullshit. I had a twin sister, Isabelle. We were as close as identical twins and we did everything together. We were even on the same Little League team. Isabelle played third base." Bobby's eyes soften as they reach back. "As teenagers, we . . . what's the right word? Vetted? We vetted each other's boyfriends and girlfriends. Is he a good guy? Is she still seeing her old boyfriend? Does he have a big mouth? The trust we had in each other was absolute. When she finally got married, I walked her down the aisle. Our father was gone by then."

This is more than I had any right to ask of him and I know it. I begin to speak, but he waves me off.

"Four hundred and thirty-three days ago, Isabelle left her Rockland County home to go to work and vanished. Women do that sometimes, when they're afraid of their husbands. They abandon their former lives altogether. That wasn't the case with Marty and Isabelle. They got along well. But even if she had a secret lover, there was nothing to prevent her from simply walking away. She had children, children she loved dearly.

"The case was handled by the State Police, but I stayed close. Isabelle's credit and debit cards were never used. No attempt was made to access her 401K, the family checking and savings accounts, or a checking account held in her name. Her car was located two months into the investigation, abandoned in Brooklyn. The only trace evidence recovered belonged to the family, including her two children and a family dog. There was no evidence of a physical attack, no blood or tissue.

"The posters went up, the website was created, the flyers were handed out. MISSING: ISABELLE KNOWLES. Her photo below, smiling that mischievous smile. Your smile, Eleni. Isabelle had your smile.

"I'm a cop, a homicide cop. I knew she was dead within two weeks. That's not—" He stops to stare at his hands. "All cops make notifications. It's part of the job and I've done my share. Sometimes it's simply that a relative has been taken to the hospital. Sometimes it's that a sister, brother, mother, daughter, father, son is dead, gone forever, no more hopes, no more dreams, wiped out. The look, Eleni, the disbelief, the sudden knowing, the horror and the wail, the awful wail. I'm a cop, of course, so I'm prepared to catch the ones who stagger and faint.

"I rarely do notifications now. Too busy with the crime scene. Uniformed officers do it. No, what I get to do is interview the family later on, after they've fully absorbed the loss, after they've walked through their homes, examined every family photo, looked into her room at an unmade bed, inhaled the lingering perfume on a cocktail dress, slipped that turquoise ring she loved on their own fingers.

"The words come by rote. First, I'm sorry for your loss. Then, do you know anyone who may have done this? Did she have any enemies? Have you noticed any strangers in the neighborhood? Can you spare a photograph? Would you make a list of her friends?

"Mostly, they break down at some point and what you want to do is take them into your arms, to protect them in some way. But you're not allowed to touch them. You have to hold it in. You have to be a professional.

"With Isabelle, I couldn't help myself, even though I knew better. I couldn't stop myself from imagining what happened to her. She wasn't killed immediately. The car was clean, remember? No, Isabelle was taken somewhere and worked on. For hours, for days? And how many ways did he, or they, find to hurt her? What instruments were used? Was she aware until the very end? Did she sense her life slipping away? Did she plead for mercy, or did she finally give up, the pain too overwhelming? Did she finally beg to be killed? I've seen the bodies, Eleni, the bodies of human beings, usually women, after days of torture. I've counted and analyzed the wounds on their bodies, scraped their blood off the walls, collected bits of their skulls, measured the bruises on their throats."

He stops suddenly, repressing a groan, then continues. "Bad as it is for me, though, it's much worse for Marty. Last week, he told me that even now, when he hears a car climbing the hill late at night, he thinks, for just a moment, that Isabelle's coming home."

I'm lying with my head against his chest, close enough to measure the beating of his heart. I try to think of something to say, but I can only come up with: "I'm sorry for your loss." As he leans over to kiss my forehead, I feel his heart rate slow.

"I stopped being able to fend it off," he says, his tone matter-of-fact now that he's finally put his heart on the line. "I'm talking about the day-to-day misery, the victims, the families, Isabelle. They're my own personal zombies. They're why so many cops kill themselves."

Bobby's hold eases. "I'm quitting," he tells me. "I've put twenty years into the job. That qualifies me for a pension and medical benefits going forward. The lieutenant knows. I told her last week. As soon as your case is resolved, I'm gonna turn in my papers."

"And do what?"

His kiss this time is more demanding. "I've got a cousin in Queens. He owns a lumber yard, and he's looking for a partner. But I'm not worried about that part."

"Then what are you worried about?"

"I'm worried about the only thing that matters, Eleni. The DNA."

CHAPTER FORTY-EIGHT
MARTHA

Halberstam's become chatty. He's somehow concluded that he and we are buddies. He can brag about the games he plays with his patients and we'll approve. There's nothing we can do about it, at least until we're free of him. But he's no longer a threat, thanks to Marshal and Kirk, and that's enough for now. True, I tend to leave his office feeling soiled (perhaps the way Eleni's supposed to feel, and never does, after a one-night, multipartner stand) but that's a small price to pay and we don't intend to miss any appointments.

Bobby's waiting for me when I turn onto South Portland Avenue, standing in front of our building, one hand jammed into his pocket, the other holding a plastic bag that can only contain a bottle of wine. He takes a moment to recognize the particular Carolyn Grand advancing toward him. Then he smiles and kisses me on the cheek.

"Hi, Martha."

Is he disappointed? Bobby's not only added Serena to his sleep mates, he's got Victoria in his sights. I joke about it with him. Sheikh Bobby and his concubines. It's gotten to the point where he's embedded so deeply in our lives it feels like he's always been there. That doesn't mean I trust him. Too many games, like our trip to the morgue. I lead him upstairs, sit him on the couch and head for the kitchen. As I open the wine, he calls out to me.

"The DNA's back, Martha."

I think he means to rattle me, but I'm not fazed. If our DNA had been found at the crime scene, we'd not only be under arrest, it would be Detective Greco come to do the arresting.

"Do I hear the rattle of handcuffs?" I call back.

He laughs but doesn't speak until I come into the living room with the wine (a pinot noir) and a couple of glasses. Then he says, "They recovered fragments of DNA at the crime scene that don't exclude you, fragments too small to be used as evidence. Seems they also don't exclude six suspects on our list, not to mention seventy or eighty thousand other city residents."

I think I'm supposed to celebrate, but something in Bobby's tone puts me off as I listen to Kirk's voice in my ear: *Don't you dare ask. Don't you dare.*

Kirk thinks we can avoid an answer, that he and Bobby can watch another baseball game or go to the bar for a drink. He thinks we can leave our questions on a dark shelf we'll never visit. I like Bobby too much—Eleni's in love with him—and we have to know. We have to.

"Do you think O'Neill did it, Bobby?"

"No, I don't."

"What about the others? The prostitutes and the pimps, one of them."

"Sorry."

I watch Bobby withdraw to a place where every atom is weighed and measured, a cop again. He's been thinking about this for a long time. Just like us.

"Let's start with the crime scene, the way it appeared when I first arrived at one thirty-seven a.m. That was before the Crime Scene Unit or a death examiner from the ME's office. I was standing in the doorway, looking into a small, dirty room. The paramedics had already pronounced the victim dead, leaving me without an excuse to enter, so I contented myself with a quick inventory. There was a table against the wall closest to me with a half-empty bottle of Jack Daniel's and an empty glass on top. A chair next to the table was covered, seat and back, with the victim's clothing. On the far wall to my left, a sink, also dirty, hung at a slight angle. To my right, the wall was broken by a secured door leading into the adjoining room."

He stops long enough to stare into my eyes for a moment, then continues. "Hank Grand was lying on a bed opposite the door. He presented as a man in late middle age, paunchy but well-muscled with tattoos on either side of his chest, one of an angel, the other a demon. Half of his body, his bare torso, was exposed, while his legs were tangled in a pair of faded green blankets. From what I could see of his head and his torso, there were no wounds on his body." He pauses long enough to glance around the room, maybe for reassurance. "Detective Greco arrived as I was standing by the door and CSU came up a few minutes after that. They cleared a path to the bed and we finally approached the body. From the foot of the bed, I counted three distinct stab wounds in the victim's back. In addition, a section of the blanket was soaked with drying blood. From the consistency of the bloodstains, I judged the victim to have been killed within the last six hours. That was the death examiner's opinion as well."

I raise a hand, and he stops speaking, his expression quizzical. I want to remind him that we lived without his presence for thirty-seven years. If necessary, we can live another thirty-seven. But I don't. I simply nod once and he continues.

"First things first, me and Greco spent the next six hours working the hotel. We were hoping the killer was close by or that at least, between the hookers, pimps and johns, we'd develop a lead. That didn't happen, but we managed to pick up a few things from the hookers and the slimeball who sits behind the desk. First thing, every bed in the hotel had a fitted sheet covering the mattress and there was a towel in every room. Neither was found in Hank Grand's room. Without doubt, they were taken because they contained trace evidence. Second, Hank Grand rented that same room every night, he and a pal named O'Neill. The pair of them, according to the hookers we questioned, were selling ten-dollar bags of heroin. The clerk also told us that Hank Grand rented the same room every night and that made the inn's regulars, all of them, potential suspects. In any event, we came to your apartment straight from the inn, mainly to do the notification. By then we knew you were—"

"Emotionally disturbed? Crazy as bedbugs?"

Bobby's expression doesn't change, though he appears tired now. He doesn't respond to my challenge, either. "Homicide cops think in terms of means, motive, and opportunity. Though it wasn't dated, the note I read most likely provided you with the opportunity. As for motive and means? You had motive aplenty and a long-bladed knife can be purchased at thousands of stores."

I finish my wine, refill the glass. "You had no right to read those messages."

"Sure, I did, but I wasn't looking for notes when I wandered around. I was looking for bloodstains. Anywhere on anything." This is ground that's already been covered and Bobby moves on without pausing. "The autopsy determined that the first stab wound passed between Hank Grand's third and fourth ribs on the left side of his body. It penetrated to a depth of seven inches, slicing through the right ventricle of his heart. This wound was fatal by itself and he probably died before the second and third strike." He turns his head to face me. "Postmortem, the front of Hank Grand's body had been washed from head to knees, probably with a disinfectant meant to clean the hotel's floors and bathrooms. No killer would do that, spend extra time with a victim, without a very good reason. I took it to mean the perpetrator expected to become a suspect and feared a DNA comparison."

Bobby's interrupted by a knock on the door. It's Marshal, who's been a good friend to us. I send him off anyway. Bobby's in the kitchen when I return. He emerges with a plate of cookies, chocolate chip, baked not from an old family recipe but from the directions on the back of a box. Bobby lays the cookies on the table and sits beside me. He begins again as though we hadn't been interrupted.

"I don't have this part in exact order, the bits and pieces that drifted in from the various labs, but here goes. Blood tests showed Hank Grand's blood-alcohol level at time of death was two point one. In addition, his blood tested positive for a significant concentration of a drug called Temazepam, which works like Valium. Between the two, according to the pathologist, Hank Grand was almost certainly unconscious and maybe comatose at the time of the attack. Then a second lab discovered traces of Temazepam on the one glass in the room, so we knew how the drug got into his system. That led us to look harder at the Golden Inn's prostitutes because robbing johns is probably the world's second-oldest profession. But we also showed your photo to everybody we questioned, which is how we dug up the witnesses. While this canvas was still in progress, our own crime lab reported that the front of the body had been thoroughly scrubbed with a highly concentrated floor cleaner, confirming the ME's impression. Thus, the initial report we received from the DNA lab came as no surprise. The lab only managed to isolate small amounts of DNA, which they were attempting to amplify." He pauses long enough to grab a cookie. "I can teach you how to bake these from scratch, Martha. If you're interested."

"I already know how. I was just too lazy. Meanwhile, you need to get back to your theory. Before I do to you what you think we did to our father. You're having too much fun, Bobby.

Especially for someone who committed what amounts to a murder."

He only smiles, but I'm not letting it go. "You didn't have to kill O'Neill," I tell him. "You could have called for backup, enough force to convince him to surrender. But you wanted him dead."

"I didn't force O'Neill to draw his weapon. Remember, he got off two shots. Murderers, as a general rule, try real hard not to get shot at."

"That's not the issue. Why you did it is the issue. Why you risked your life to protect us and why you're here, sounding like a prosecutor making his closing argument."

Bobby shakes his head. Not now. "The blood we observed on the blankets originated on the side of the blankets closest to Hank Grand's body. Most likely, the perpetrator used the blankets to wipe the knife blade as it was withdrawn, eliminating potential blood spatter. Personally, I think Hank Grand's murderer came away clean, closing off that avenue of investigation."

I watch him pop the cookie he's been holding between two fingers into his mouth, the wafer at some crazy cop communion.

"It's pretty obvious," he continues, "to me if not my partner, that the killing was carefully planned, from the initial contact to the cleanup. Oh, and one thing I failed to mention. I ran into a prostitute who works from inside the hotel. Seems there's something of a brothel on the second floor. She told me that she knocked on Hank Grand's door at nine o'clock that night and nobody answered. So, you got lucky, too, lucky you weren't interrupted, that nobody got a good look at your face."

I shake my head. It's the wrong time for a detour. "What about Greco? What did he think?"

"He was too focused on O'Neill and the pimps to get it. But there's no way O'Neill or some anonymous pimp would stick around long enough to clean the body or carry away the sheet and the towel. Or for that matter, to carefully drape two blankets over an unconscious man to eliminate blood spatter. Your IQ, by the way, is one thirty-five. O'Neill's is eighty-eight."

I'm listening for advice, but my brother and sisters aren't talking. Maybe that's because there's nothing to say. "I assume you've got a theory of how it all went down."

"More like a movie."

"And who's the star?"

"We need to start earlier than that, Martha. It's not all that easy to make a plan if you don't know who's going to show up when the time comes to run it. This implies an element of control, don't you think?" He stares at me for a minute, then smiles. "Last chance to confess."

"No go, Bobby. I'm stickin' to my story. We're innocent. You got the wrong psychotic."

"Alright, have it your way." His smile fades, and his eyes turn inward. "I don't think your father expected you to show up. Not after all those years. Most likely, he was playing with you, like claiming he wanted to reconcile. Psychopaths love to manipulate. But he had to be worried about having his parole violated, too. Believe me, it doesn't take much, not for a convicted pedophile, and Hank Grand, after twenty-seven years in the system, had to know it. So, when you arrived, he would have been on his guard, suspecting, maybe, that you'd come to set a trap. Meanwhile, you're carrying the Temazepam, already ground up, maybe in a pill bottle. How do you get it from the bottle into his body? Not while he's watching. Not while he's standing there, wondering what to make of you. No, you came there to kill him, no matter the personal cost, no matter how much it hurt, and so you took him to bed, knowing he wouldn't resist. What happened then? Already drunk, maybe he fell asleep for a few minutes. In fact, in my movie, you carry the spiked drink to his bed. You wait until he sits up, then hand the glass to him. 'Here, Daddy, you must be awful thirsty.'"

"You're a bastard, Bobby."

"What can I say? I'm a cop and bastard is what cops do."

"That doesn't give you the right to dissect us. We're not specimens."

His expression momentarily softens, but his tone remains firm. "It's the planning that impresses me the most. Who was going to go in first? And who would be kept in the dark, like Serena? Me, I don't believe that Serena just happened to be present when Greco knocked on the door. Serena was sent forth to do battle precisely because she was defenseless, because she wasn't armed with the truth. Likewise for the identity—God, how I hate that word—who knocked on Hank Grand's door. She had to be carefully chosen. For sure, it couldn't be you or Kirk, no way. As for Serena, leaving the interrogation aside, she's far too timid. She could never bring it off. And try to imagine fastidious Victoria stripping out of her dress. Imagine her displaying herself for a moment before reaching out to touch Daddy's flesh."

It's like Bobby's inside me, opening doors, and I don't like it. I'm thinking about relief, but there's no relief coming.

"Eleni would be the obvious choice. But Eleni has this habit of only sleeping with men she wants to sleep with. Could she fake that attraction with her father? Make him feel comfortable? Eleni is the most fearless among you, but she has no guile, and game plans are far from her strong suit. No, Eleni wouldn't do and that leaves—"

"Tina."

"No, not Tina. Carolyn Grand went to the Golden Inn that night. She knew her daddy better than he knew himself and she had murder in her heart. Already drunk, Hank Grand never had a chance. This was his most sordid prison fantasy come to life. Yes, Daddy. No, Daddy. I'll be good, Daddy. Do you think Eleni could pull that off?"

I stand up and walk to the window, just as if there were something I really want to look at. No, I can't imagine Eleni saying those words. I can't imagine anyone saying them. Nor do I want to. At the same time, I know they must have been said.

"Once your father was unconscious, Carolyn laid both blankets over his back, then straddled him, her torso above his hips. Most first-time killers hesitate at this point. The initial wound is usually the most shallow. Carolyn, by contrast, raised the knife above her head and drove it straight down with all her might. As a matter of pure luck, it passed between two ribs and Hank Grand bled out in less than a minute. If the knife had been driven into a rib, on the other hand, the tip would probably have broken off and Carolyn would've had a really pissed Hank Grand in her face. But it wasn't. The blade went in clean. The essential goal was accomplished. Now for the cleanup."

I know I'm wasting my time, but I can't help myself. "How can you think that Tina, after everything—"

"Martha, there is no Tina. The being you call Tina is what's left of Carolyn Grand."

"I just don't understand how you can believe that Tina, and I'll call her that until the day I cease to exist, could—"

Again he stops me. "I think Carolyn Grand is the bravest human being I've ever known. She protected her brood and I admire her tremendously. And there's no use pretending anymore. You were all she had, you and Kirk and Eleni and Victoria and Serena. Insane? Four pretend children living in the same body? I don't give a shit, Martha. I only know that she stood up to the monster who took her childhood. And the revenge she sought and got? It was for all of you, just as her remembering was for all of you."

A minute passes, then another. Bobby wants me to speak first, but I won't. Finally, he gives up. "Carolyn wouldn't know a toilet cleaner from dishwashing liquid. She didn't sanitize the scene. She called in a self-described drudge named Martha. And it worked. You were thorough enough to prevent a positive ID, but we both know who killed Hank Grand and it wasn't Alfred O'Neill or some broke hooker who needed a fix. The fatal blow came from the hand of Carolyn Grand. You became an accessory when you cleaned up."

I stare into his eyes. Cop or friend? There's a question out there, waiting to be asked, but I can't manage to say the words as I watch him pour the last of the wine into our glasses. I can't speak, but I have to speak.

"Let's say you've got it right, every detail. What are you going to do about it?"

"Do you still think I'd hurt you, Martha?"

"Just answer the question. What are you going to do?"

"Nothing. Nothing I want to do and nothing I can do. That's because there's no evidence to back my theory. Greco can't even prove that you left your apartment on the night your father was killed. No, everybody's agreed, Ford, Greco, and myself. We're gonna put the murder on Alfred O'Neill."

"How do you explain the cleanup afterward?"

"Hank Grand's body was sanitized with a floor cleaner used by the hotel. There are gallon jugs in cleaning closets on every floor. As for why . . ." Ortega's thin smile broadens. He's tickled about something. "This'll blow your mind. Greco's working theory for the past month is that your father and O'Neill were lovers in prison. And why not? Both men were serving long sentences, both had committed sex crimes in the past and they definitely knew each other while they were incarcerated. So, according to Greco, it was O'Neill who needed to destroy DNA evidence."

Bobby stops for a moment, but I find myself with nothing to say. "If it sounds stupid, that's because it is. So what?

We don't have enough hard evidence to convict O'Neill at trial. Or even to secure an indictment. But O'Neill's dead, so there won't be a trial. He's guilty because we say he is. In the cop business, we call this exceptional clearance. As in exceptionally good for the bosses." Bobby leans forward to gently touch the back of my hand. "Hey, you wanna hear a cop's definition of a perfect murder?"

"Sure."

"A perfect murder is any murder you get away with." Bobby raises his glass, waits until I join him, then says, without a trace of irony: "Here's to perfect murders and perfect victims."

CHAPTER FORTY-NINE

MARTHA

It's nine o'clock and Bobby's seated on our loveseat. He's sitting next to Marshal, who's brought his bong and a bud of hydroponic weed. I've indulged, which I rarely do. Just as well. We're watching an incredibly stupid movie, *Dumb and Dumber.* Sober, I'd be long gone. But now we're laughing our heads off, me and the boys. There's an open box of pastries lying on the seat of the wooden chair we're using for a coffee table. An empty bottle of low-end Korbel champagne sits in the sink, awaiting a quick rinse. I'm at our little table, sorting laundry. Ours and Bobby's.

I should be pissed because it's bad enough that I have to clean up after my sisters. True, Bobby's paying for much of the food we eat. True, he bought the champagne and the pastries. Tough shit. We need to reach an understanding of just who and what he is to us. Because now that I've had a chance to think it over, he's become a mystery once again. Did Bobby protect us? Or was he, like his partner, merely unable to establish probable cause for an arrest?

Eleni won't care, Kirk either. But Serena, who continues to embrace the good in all of us, will surely want resolution.

Likewise Victoria, despite having taken him to bed. Victoria is eternally wary, eternally pessimistic. Our sky is always falling. And there's real danger in embracing a lifestyle we can never afford on our own.

We're watching the scene where Jim Carrey is ripped off by an old lady on a motorized cart. I'm now seeing each scene as self-contained. Scene following scene like railroad cars with no bumpers between them. Story of our lives, right?

Or maybe not. For the last five hours I've been returning to Bobby's speech, which I'm sure was carefully calculated. A matter of a cop's instinct never to show his whole hand. How convenient, Serena being at home when Greco knocked on the door. Totally ignorant Serena, who could tell him nothing. And me, in that hotel exactly when I was needed. Because the cop was right. Tina could remember to bring the knife and the Temazepam. And, yes, she could drive that knife into his heart with all the force at her command. But the aftermath belonged to me. And it's only through blind luck that I found a cleaning cart standing in the hall. That I was able, no matter how repulsed, to cleanse my dead father's flesh. I remember fighting an urge to vomit as I gathered the sheets and my daddy's semen-stained underwear. As I dumped both, along with the knife, in an industrial dumpster half full of construction debris. I climbed into that dumpster, dug down almost to the bottom, buried the evidence in something too slimy to think about. And when I finally got home, I stood in the shower until my skin began to peel away.

There's Victoria, too, at the review board hearing. Appropriately dressed Victoria with her always-appropriate demeaner. How convenient. And how convenient her visits to the many agencies when we first applied for benefits. And wasn't it demure Victoria who kept our first appointment with Halberstam? Wasn't it Victoria who sat for those job interviews? Saying all the right things? Smiling in all the right places?

Bobby's outside, asleep on the couch. I'm lying in bed, listening to the bass line from some moronic rap tune. Courtesy of a giant SUV double-parked across the street. *Bum, bum, bum*, pause. *Bum, bum, bum*, pause. Over and over again. Loud enough to vibrate the hairs on the back of my neck. Just now, I'm hoping for a drive-by.

I'm wearing my usual bedtime gear, boxer shorts and a sleeveless white T-shirt. I raise my knees and stare for a moment at my thighs. They're Eleni's thighs, Serena's thighs, even Kirk's thighs. I find myself asking a series of questions asked by every therapist unfortunate enough to have us for a patient. Where do I go when I'm not in control of our body? Who am I when I live in a realm called oblivion? Where was I before I came back?

Most of all, who or what chooses?

I walk into the bathroom, stand before the mirror and stare into my own eyes. Trying, maybe, to see into my brain.

No, that's wrong. To see into *our* brain, like our thighs, our teeth, our fucking toenails. But somewhere behind my eyes, somewhere in that brain, a collection of neurons decides our moment-to-moment fate.

The other options? Possession by a demon from the spirit world? Space aliens from the dark side of the moon?

Tucked into some dark corner of our brain and surrounded by the billions of neurons that control every bodily function, those few neurons aren't about to wave hello. But it occurs to me as I raise my fingers to trace the lines of my face, that maybe they aren't unthinking. Maybe they can detect ongoing threats. Maybe, like children, they know when to stop fooling around, to get serious, to survive. Maybe they argue among themselves before they reach a decision. Maybe they debate when to make a change, who to put in charge, the whys and wherefores of the particular abyss at our feet.

If I'm not real, how can I want so much to simply live? If I pinch myself, do I hurt, do we hurt, or does only Carolyn Grand hurt? Then I fart and instantly feel my sisters surround me. Kirk, Eleni, Serena, Victoria holding a nose she doesn't have. Somehow, I expect them to comfort me. Instead they're laughing.

Kirk's telling me about an after-hours bar where desperate housewives pursue the perverted desires they've held at bay throughout their lives. Eleni's more direct. She's already spoken to Bobby. If I want, he'll find a woman, bring her home and spend the night at his own apartment. Serena's humming a tuneless tune that could only have been composed in the Far East. She strokes my hair, a touch I both can and can't feel. Victoria's demanding that I suck it up the way Serena sucked it up when Greco came calling. Even Bobby chimes in. From his bed on the couch, he begins to snore.

I walk up to our single bedroom window, pull back the curtain and stare at the Escalade parked across the street. At the greedy hands reaching through its windows. Then I'm laughing, roaring, holding my sides, maybe for the first time in the half-life that defines my existence. Every therapist, the good and the bad, wanted to heal us, to remake us in their image. And now I'm thinking that at least it won't hurt. When the remake finally happens. One day I'll leave the body, believing myself secure, and never return. But at least it won't hurt.

ABOUT THE AUTHOR

A.F. Carter lives, works and writes in New York City.